GIFTS OF HONEY

GIFTS OF HONEY

(4th in the Bachelor Preacher Mystery Series)

BOB WYATT

authorHOUSE®

AuthorHouse™
1663 Liberty Drive
Bloomington, IN 47403
www.authorhouse.com
Phone: 1-800-839-8640

© 2011 by Bob Wyatt. All rights reserved.

No part of this book may be reproduced, stored in a retrieval system, or transmitted by any means without the written permission of the author.

First published by AuthorHouse   10/28/2011

ISBN: 978-1-4670-3790-7 (sc)
ISBN: 978-1-4670-4067-9 (ebk)

Library of Congress Control Number: 2011917131

Printed in the United States of America

Any people depicted in stock imagery provided by Thinkstock are models, and such images are being used for illustrative purposes only.
Certain stock imagery © Thinkstock.

This book is printed on acid-free paper.

Because of the dynamic nature of the Internet, any web addresses or links contained in this book may have changed since publication and may no longer be valid. The views expressed in this work are solely those of the author and do not necessarily reflect the views of the publisher, and the publisher hereby disclaims any responsibility for them.

CHAPTER ONE

When I graduated from Santa Anna Biblical Studies College in Santa Anna, California, I felt totally prepared to preach and work in the pulpit ministry. The classes on preparing sermons had been helpful in demonstrating the three point message style and provided some helpful shortcuts in developing them. The faculty members had handed out stacks of illustrations to use and complimentary books of sermon outlines. It didn't take long to organize and prepare a 20 minute sermon after taking the classes and having these materials. I could do this fulltime pulpit ministry job with ease, but it bothered me that it was this easy and something did not seem quite right.

After thinking about the quality of the sermons, I decided that my messages were not spirit filled nor did they come from the heart as long as I used the pre-packaged method. The sermons had about as much flavor as frozen TV dinners prepared in the microwave. Soon I turned to reading the Bible carefully. I examined several commentaries, and sought to feel the message in my heart before preaching on Sunday morning. I was convinced with this approach that the people would be compelled to be in church. Those that were lost would come forward and every Sunday new people would be saved.

"This is my mission and why I was called to preach," I mistakenly thought. "My sermons will bring the people to God."

Ah yes, youth. How excited we get when we think we are on the right track. It was a noble idea mixed with a bit of over confidence and ego, but once in the actual pulpit position reality took over. I found it wasn't just on Sunday morning that a message was needed. There was a Sunday night sermon, a sermon at a nursing home Sunday afternoon, another sermon for a funeral *or wedding or both or sometimes several in a week. There was Wednesday night Bible study and a Sunday school lesson to prepare. I soon found that there wasn't enough time to dig deep into the Scripture for all of the needed presentations.*

I got annoyed when people interrupted me during Bible study. I thought, "How do you expect me to preach a powerful sermon on Sunday when you keep taking me away from the Bible?"

Frustrated I turned to prayer and thought back to Bible College. Pulling out my notebooks from classes I searched for advice on how to manage my time better in order to get all those sermons and lessons prepared. After a few hours of examination it was apparent that the reason the professors had provided the sermon outlines and illustrations was for this very purpose. I don't remember them saying anything directly about the number of sermons that would be expected, but it was obvious that the providing of so much material by them was the anticipated need that would come once on the field and in the pulpit ministry.

Thinking about all of the handouts brought me right back to the pre-packaged sermon again, but it was different now. I understood what the faculty meant. I remembered one faculty member saying, "It is important to feel the message and have it come from the heart. Selecting your illustrations carefully will help do that."

That same professor encouraged me to carry a notebook to jot ideas for sermons or experiences that could be used as examples later. It was a good idea and I was amazed at how quickly it became a source for sermon illustrations. These illustrations helped to make the sermon real and a part of me and enabled me to preach from the heart.

Another faculty member suggested the use of a few jokes to keep the interest and to approach tough subjects with a bit of humor. At the time I thought that would give the impression that I wasn't serious about the message or topic. Experience showed otherwise and it turned out to be good advice. With many sermons every week there was a need for fresh ideas and approaches. With a joke here and there it breathed a little fresh air into an otherwise stuffy sermon.

Following a joke in one sermon, it occurred to me that sermons were a form of entertainment. As I watched the people in front of me laughing, punching each other with a nod and smiling, it occurred to me that people want to be happy and filled with good thoughts.

In preparing the next sermon I concentrated on writing a shorter and funnier sermon. I searched joke books for things that were meaningful yet funny and shaped the direction of the writing in a direction which allowed me to include a particularly funny joke. The sermon was packed with line after line of humor. In the midst of preaching I came full circle and realized I had been tricked by the devil. In the midst of the laughing and entertainment the message of Christ was lost.

No matter when, where, why or what the occasion, the focus in the message must be that Jesus saves and that Christ is the Savior for a world of lost sinners. The invitation must be "Come to Him today."

Preaching on Sundays is obviously a major function of the preacher, but stepping away from the pulpit and walking into the work week is when the real ministry begins. There is visiting the sick and the elderly; attending the various community functions where ministers are expected to be in attendance; organizing and participating in rallies, workshops, conventions, camps, vacation Bible school; and traveling to other communities to attend meetings. All of these call upon the minister and drain him of energy he would rather spend on preparing the Sunday morning sermon.

During a typical minister's day, the preacher will ride emotions like a roller coaster. One minute he finds himself with a group celebrating the birth of a child and a few seconds later with another group mourning the death of a relative or friend. He oversees the union of a couple and a minute later cries inside his heart as he watches a couple separate over finances and children and religion. He sees abused, neglected children sitting with arguing parents that claim they don't understand why their children have become troublemakers while they cuss and slap each other with cold remarks. The life of a minister is rather a remarkable one.

Looking at some of the other preachers in the area I noticed most were married and had children. "There was not enough time to get the church work done as it was," I thought to myself. "To spend time being a good father, attending the various activities that the children are involved and volunteering for the various organizations like scouts, 4-H, PTA, etc. would overwhelm me."

I questioned, "How do they do that and still remain strong and inspiring in the pulpit? How does a minister be a leader for the church and also an inspirational father for his family and a good husband for his wife? How do preachers handle all that pressure?"

As I graduated from Bible College I looked forward to having my own congregation and had visions of anticipated growth in attendance and weekly additions to the church. I looked forward to hosting rallies, workshops, speaking at conventions and being used by God in a wonderful way. Yes, I thought I was prepared by the school and was ready to tackle whatever challenges came my way, but reality set in that first Sunday when lightning struck the parsonage and I watched everything I owned go up in smoke. All the commentaries, school notes, jokes and illustrations were gone. I was stripped of all my packaged solutions I thought would make me a great minister.

Yet, from the ashes of disaster came God's demonstration of what he wanted me to do. Within minutes Dollie Burgess had me moved into her spare room. Ike Skelton called and invited me to have Sunday dinner with him and his wife at Porter's Place. Steve Elsea brought a bedroom set, Marlene a chair, Maggie a table, and the Preachers' Alliance a new Bible with three commentaries. These were good people filled with the Christian Spirit. They witnessed to me that first week more than I could witness to them for a full year.

My powerful sermons to shake them up and lead them to Salvation; my ideas of how to achieve record attendance and baptisms; my humor to entertain them so they would want to be in service every Sunday; my example to follow to make the congregation better in line were gone in seconds with a fire. The whole incident had me feeling small and unprepared.

After one week in my first fulltime ministry I quickly recognized how lacking in the Spirit I was. My life was not worth anything when it came to saving people. In reality, I could not save them. It was Christ who died and conquered death. It was Christ whose blood was shed for our sins. That is the message to be shared and remembered. Jesus Saves!

Josh McDowell, editor of the local newspaper, stopped by the church to interview me about the fire. More importantly he came by to welcome me to Sassafras Springs and to give me encouragement. Since that first visit we have been good friends. Although he is not a member of the congregation, like a brother he comes by to check on me. When he sees I am depressed he just about always has the right word to say.

On that first occasion he explained and shared examples about what a giving community Sassafras Springs is and encouraged me to allow the people of the congregation to work and share in the ministry of the church. Josh noted that the mission of the minister is to navigate the ship (church) through the worldly waters by encouraging those rowing and helping to keep the church *moving forward. He emphasized the importance of having everyone work together and stressed to let them do their jobs when they volunteer or are asked to do something without interfering. He encouraged letting the volunteers do the task their way letting them shine their lights to glorify Christ and to give them space to do the will of God as He wants rather than as the minister wants.*

He said, "It is not the preacher's job to head every committee or every class or every project. Each member has an ability to do their part. Make sure they know it and are invited to share in the ministry."

My heart was pounding as I stared at the people around me in the restaurant. There was Dollie, Ike, Josh, Steve and others—total strangers a week ago who had provided assistance to me. Like sweet honey, they sweetened my life that seemed destroyed with the fire and made it a rich delicious dessert. I had never felt this way before. I suddenly felt a part of something very important as dependence and appreciation replaced my independence and arrogance.

The town that was known for giving gifts of honey to each other in the form of kindness continued to come to my rescue in dozens of special ways that following week. I had come to help them but they had helped me. God had shown me very quickly in my first ministry that church members care and strengthen each other.

My name is Jack Temple and I'm the minister at the Nickerson Street Church in Sassafras Springs, Missouri. Steve Elsea, chairman of the church board, had taken me to enjoy a meal at the new Chinese Restaurant at the mall on the south side of town. We talked about my possibly coming to Sassafras Springs. The next Sunday I shook his hand in a booth at Porter's Place while eating one of Ike's delicious pastries and became a fulltime minister for the first time.

It was a huge undertaking I began to realize as I drove around town looking at the community, observing the kids playing in the park, the elderly sitting in front of the nursing home, the people eating at the fast food place called the Crème Maid.

"So where do I begin?" I questioned that day.

Over the past few years, I have noted ministers struggling. There are apparent hidden dangers the minister faces. He can be consumed by the amount of the work load. He can be driven to think he is alone in the battle for Christ. He can place his confidence in himself as he begins to see those failing around him. He can lose his faith and serve only to get a paycheck. He may put himself on a pinnacle thinking everyone should follow his example. At this point he has lost the vision of Christ and the mission for which he has been called.

It is a critical error made by ministers when they fail to see and use the abilities of their membership. The members are a vital part of the church. These are people that are there to strengthen the minister by their witness and example if the minister stops to see them. They are the ones who will bring their neighbors, relatives and friends to participate in the church family. This produces the growth the minister mistakenly thinks will happen because of his sermons and calling program.

"The task at hand for the minister is helping others help others," said Josh the editor of the newspaper.

That second week after the fire I continued to learn—from the 95 year old lady in the nursing home when she gave me a hot pad she had made from scraps of material; from the farmer in the field who got off his tractor and filled a bucket with ears of corn to take home; from the boy on the pond bank fishing who offered me a pole and gave me a moment of quiet meditation during a day that had been fast paced; and from the newspaper boy who sent a newspaper crashing into my room when it hit the window . . . who offered to mow the yard to pay for the window. All of these individuals were witnessing about Christ—not me witnessing to them, but them witnessing to me.

There was the mother with six small children struggling to get groceries to the car who stopped to give me a pleasant "hello" and smile. I in return stopped and helped her to the car and told some jokes to the children to bring smiles to their faces.

This is how to make the world a better place. This is how our lives become more meaningful and useful. This is how we become special witnesses of Christ in our communities.

An example of this is Roger Brown. He is one of the members of the Nickerson Street Church and although he is not one of the most outwardly dedicated members of the local congregation he is involved in serving Christ in numerous ways The stories behind his façade are varied and filled with adventure—yes, and mystery.

"Sir," began Roger Brown as he explained his plan to the teller at the Bank of Sassafras Springs, "I want to send this money to Nigeria."

Travis Lowry, the teller, looked at the check and then at Roger. Shaking his head, the teller sat the check down between the two of them. The teller leaned forward and whispered to Roger and then leaned back.

"What did you say?" Roger Brown asked with a puzzled look on his face. "I didn't hear you. Would you repeat that and why are you whispering?"

Travis Lowry shrugged his shoulders as he looked toward the office of the president of the bank, Barbara Edwina Stegner. The office was empty. The teller's gaze moved to the vice president's office, Brenda Gardner. Again he found no one available. As the teller looked across the room he gave a sigh of relief when Rev. Jack Temple entered the bank. The teller frantically motioned with a wave and a sign for the preacher to join Roger and the teller.

"A hearty good morning to the both of you," greeted Rev. Jack Temple. "This is turning out to be a great day. I heard the weather report this morning predicting hail and thunderstorms and well—," he said as he pointed to the sunshiny day outside.

"It does look like a great day, Rev. Temple," said Travis Lowry, "and welcome to the bank."

"Good morning Rev. Temple," said Roger Brown. "I have some business I would like to discuss with you. I am coming into some money and thought that you would want to know that the addition to the church can be built as soon as the money arrives. I plan to donate a million dollars."

"Roger!" exclaimed Rev. Temple. "That is wonderful news."

Rev. Jack Temple was stunned at Roger's remarks, but tried not to show it. He had never thought about the financial situation of Roger and had never considered that Roger might donate a million dollars to the church building fund. Rev. Temple felt embarrassed as he looked at Roger. Jack realized he knew practically nothing about this generous church member in front of him. Rev. Temple didn't even know where Roger lived or what he had done in life or anything about him except that he was the last to get to church before services started and the first to leave at the "Amen" of the closing prayer.

"Was there a death in the family?" questioned Rev. Temple with deep concern in his voice.

Roger ignored the question and launched into his plans for the building. He explained how he hoped an activity room for the young people would be included. He explained how when he was growing up he needed a place at church to get together with friends. He was excited about providing a "Christian" place for young people to go after school or after basketball games. He then promised to purchase video games and other equipment to make it special and fun for the young people.

"But you need to know the most important part, Rev. Temple," said Travis Lowry as he handed Roger's personal check to Jack for examination. "Roger is preparing to wire this money to the people who are supposedly sending him 3 million dollars. The ten thousand dollar check is to cover the costs of settling the will for this person they claim has left Roger the money in Nigeria."

"You are sending them a ten thousand dollar check? Sending it to Nigeria?" asked Rev. Temple with his mouth wide open in shock.

Rev. Temple looked at the teller who winked and made a motion with his head toward Roger Brown to signal the need for some advice to be given to Roger. Rev. Temple looked at Travis with a questioned look and then turned toward Roger's smiling face. Rev. Temple took the check in his hand and looked at it and cleared his throat. He paused and then looked straight at Roger.

"Don't you want to talk to Roger?" asked Travis Lowry. "Someone needs to let him know as he can't afford to lose $10,000."

"Yes, something about this doesn't sound right. Ah, Roger," began Rev. Temple. "Have you ever heard of this guy that died and left you the money?"

Roger squirmed a bit. A frown came on his face as he stuttered and tried to explain to Rev. Temple that he was not to tell anyone about the details.

"You don't know him do you?" continued Rev. Temple. "The fact is this came in an email from someone you don't know and has said someone you don't know has left you 3 million dollars. Do I have it right?"

Roger Brown looked at the floor. He groaned with embarrassment. Hearing Rev. Temple say what had happened made him realize it couldn't be true. Roger started to leave when Rev. Temple touched his shoulder and looked at Roger with compassion.

"Roger, look at me," remarked Rev. Temple. "Your heart was in the right place. You didn't want the money out of greed. You just wanted to help others. I congratulate you in your desire to help others. I have not known you very well, but I can see that you are a caring person. I have to tell you this is a scam. There are thousands of them on the internet. Sending them this money would have hurt you financially wouldn't it?"

"Yes," replied Roger Brown. "I was thinking the money I got back would ease my financial condition and possibly have enabled me to get a powered scooter to use instead of this wheelchair. It's tough these days since I lost the use of my legs. In this wheelchair people don't see me. When I go by people look away or look another direction. I'm just someone rolling by or sitting helplessly nearby. I hear things and see things that most don't. And yes, I saw a chance to do something I have wanted to do for a couple of years. I recognize the need for a youth center in this town every day. I see the groups of young people wandering the streets and hear what they are talking about. I know trouble can only be minutes away when the young people are not guided in the proper direction. It just seemed like God was providing the opportunity."

"God knows your heart," continued Rev. Temple, "but you know this is a scam. You have to be careful on the internet all the time. The scams all sound good. Some are just for $100 promising you millions but it is all a trick. $100 doesn't seem like much but when these evil people get a hundred people to respond it makes a nice little bundle."

"And I was willing to send the whole amount it would have taken 100 dummies to send. That makes me really, really, really stupid."

"No, it just shows you care a lot about people and want to help them," Rev. Temple stated. "Think about it. I have a problem of wanting to help everyone around me. I was drilled the lesson of the 'Good Samaritan' in the Bible by my family. It is like I am powerless at times to keep from doing something I think is needed. I still pick up hitchhikers despite the fact I know they may kill me or rob me. I talk to everyone around me despite some of them not being honest. The message of the Good Samaritan dominates my life."

"Yes," began Travis Lowry, "but that is what we like about you Rev. Temple. You are constantly finding ways of helping people. Your congregation has taken up the 'cross' and are changing the way people think in this community. We have in fact become a community of caring people. Not everyone is caring though as there are some who like to take advantage of those of us who are willing to help others. Thankfully, more are taking time to help the little old lady cross the street or help get a child home that has wandered too far away from his yard."

"That's the spirit," interrupted Rev. Temple. "Everyone needs to be looking for the opportunity to help others."

"So, what if this money is intended to help others? Maybe I should send my check so we can use the money for the good in the community like we were talking about?" stated Roger Brown.

"Roger," quickly replied Rev. Temple, "you got lost again in dreams and are not looking at reality. This is a scam. No matter how much you want to use the money for helping others it still will not come to you. They just want YOUR money."

"Oh yeah," sighed Roger Brown. "The email seemed so sincere, caring and eager to help others and it said I had been picked to help spread the man's money in doing worthwhile projects all over the world. It was to be his last act of goodness."

"They are liars saying the worst lies and even include talk about Jesus and doing good things to get your attention and sympathies," added Rev. Temple. "I get them all the time on my computer too."

"You don't?" remarked Roger Brown and Travis Lowry together.

"Yes," replied Rev. Temple.

"I would like to see some of them" requested Roger Brown. "It would help to see what you have gotten. I need you to explain how to tell if they are scams or not. That will make me feel a little better. Yes, I know that is silly, but I really do want to know how you can tell mine is a scam. It seems so real—like I was picked by God to do this special thing and it hurts to think it was all a trick by someone across the ocean in Nigeria."

"It may not be in Nigeria," continued Rev. Temple. "It may be someone right here in town. You never know where they are. They work on our emotions and rip us off without the least bit of guilt."

"Pardon me for interrupting," began Dollie Burgess as she joined the group. "Jack, did you remember to take those donuts to the VBS planning meeting?"

Rev. Temple looked at her with surprise. "What donuts?"

Dollie lifted the lid on the box she was carrying. Inside could be seen the glistening icing on top of the strawberry flavored treats. Other bank employees began moving closer as they smelled the delicious scent of the freshly baked donuts. Dollie nodded "no" to them with a smile as she handed them to Rev. Temple and repeated so the employees would hear, "These are for the VBS teachers' meeting."

"Wait a minute," he said as he yanked his head around. "What VBS meeting?"

"Oh dear," continued Dollie Burgess. "You didn't see my note on the refrigerator. Maggie called a VBS meeting this morning to discuss possible missions to support during the summer's Vacation Bible School.

I'm sorry I didn't tell you in person. Here are the donuts I had setting on the counter for you to take. If you hurry you may have enough time to get to the meeting."

"Roger," said Rev. Temple turning his attention back to Roger Brown. "Meet me at the church office at noon and I'll show you some examples of scams online."

Roger nodded approval and started rolling his wheel chair to the front door of the bank.

"In fact," added Rev. Temple, "I'll order a Super Supreme Pizza from Roselee's Pizza Parlor. Have you had one? They are fantastic. Do you like black olives?"

"I like olives and anchovies," replied Roger Brown as he turned back toward Rev. Temple, "but have never eaten at Roselee's."

"Be at my church office at noon," concluded Rev. Temple as he headed for the door too. "I'll have a pizza ordered for us to enjoy during the noon hour while I show you scams on the computer."

Roger Brown was eager to have one of the Super Supreme's from Roselee's Pizza Parlor as he had heard about them for a long time. Being in a wheelchair prevented him from going to the restaurant as it was too far from his place unless he planned to be gone the whole day.

Travis Lowry watched as Rev. Temple rushed off to the VBS meeting, Dollie Burgess made a deposit of her social security check at another teller's window and Roger wheeled out the door and on to the walk. Travis thought about what a terrible thing it would have been if Roger had wired $10,000 to Nigeria. He felt good having helped to avert a scam.

CHAPTER TWO

"All in favor say 'Aye'?" asked Maggie Cushing as she forced the Vacation Bible School faculty to a decision. "Opposed 'No'?"

The group of women represented an excellent group of teachers. There was Rachel Parkhurst, "Teacher of the Year" two years ago at Sassafras Springs R-II Elementary. She taught the Kindergarten and had a reputation of being firm but fun and knew how to make students excited about being in school. She was the perfect teacher to start a youngster. After two years of persuasion, Director Maggie Cushing had managed to enlist Rachel to teach the 4 & 5 year old class.

Taking the task of the 1st & 2nd grade class was Emily Houseman. She had retired from teaching but always enjoyed the opportunity to work with this age group. Her specialty was finger plays. Each closing program for VBS featured her group using sign language to share favorite memory verses.

Teacher for the Middler Class of 3rd & 4th graders was Colleen Marx. Known as a disciplinarian at the local school she usually lightened up during VBS. She normally taught Jr. High Math and had found early in her teaching career that to handle Junior High Students a teacher needed to be firm and consistent in the rules and regulations. On the other hand, for a week with 3rd & 4th graders, she found being a little laid back and more relaxed was more successful.

Junior Class teacher for the 5ᵗʰ & 6ᵗʰ graders was Sarah Jenkins, a young good looking woman who had won the hearts of her students year after year with her singing in class. The group was always led in doing special musical tributes to Bible heroes and would share some of this music on stage in the closing program. Sarah's smile gave a lift to all who came in contact with her. During the church service the previous Sunday the 5ᵗʰ & 6ᵗʰ graders were eagerly asking if Ms. Jenkins would be back as teacher and expressed joy that she had accepted.

Taking charge of the Jr. High Class of 7ᵗʰ & 8ᵗʰ graders was Steve Elsea. He planned to close his hardware store early so that he could be at the church building a couple of hours before the opening exercises started. He wanted to be sure his lesson plans and the craft materials would be in place so the class work and activities would go like clockwork. Steve, a perfectionist, wanted to be sure each night would be stimulating, challenging and meaningful.

As an added incentive for this age to attend VBS, he provided special crafts. This year's projects were things the students would be able to keep for years to come. One project was building a bookcase or a night stand. There were beautiful plaster of Paris molds to paint as plaques for the wall. Another was a bird house kit. Owning the hardware store Steve Elsea was able to provide the materials and tools necessary for the advanced projects.

The pre-school teachers were Lori Calder and Linda Morrow. They had a repertoire of games and fun activities that would keep the younger crowd busy and entertained as the lessons would be shared. Calder and Morrow worked together extremely well. They also handled this age group in the Sunday school and had developed an outreach program to the parents. Their success had been praised by Rev. Temple and shared at the Show Me Rally in Moberly at Central Christian College of the Bible as a workshop.

Mary Lynn Sumner volunteered to oversee the refreshments each night with the assistance of Mrs. Julie Ferguson, the +90 year old neighbor of Dollie Burgess and Rev. Temple. Mary Lynn had surprised everyone last year with treats that were not only delicious but nutritious. The raw vegetables included carrots, radishes, tomatoes, celery and potatoes that had been shaped into flowers or interesting designs. The kids loved them and were fighting over the last ones on the platters provided to each classroom. Sugarless fruit juices were the delicious drinks. Sliced apples, oranges, watermelon, strawberries and grapes were included as well.

Music director was Joan Stacy who invited some guitar players and a pretty good trap set player, Jay Shaffner, to back up the singing for the VBS. It had been a tremendous success last year with the students learning the new Bible verse songs quickly and energetically. Sherrie Bennett provided accompaniment at the piano in the ensemble.

The eight teachers paused in their voting as they turned to see who was entering the room. The breeze from the open door lifted the tablecloth on the refreshment table and sent papers flying off the center table. The ladies quickly jumped and scurried around picking up their notes. Rev. Temple blushed and looked embarrassed as he walked briskly to the refreshment table, smoothed the wrinkles out on the cloth, and sat the box of donuts down.

"So what have you decided?" Rev. Temple began as he rotated to face the group. "Bring me up to date on the plans."

He was startled when he turned to see all eight women pointing at the box of donuts. He laughed and handed the box to Maggie Cushing. She opened the box and released the delicious smell of fresh baked donuts. Everyone responded with an "hmmmmm" sound as they reached to help themselves.

"I can guess where these came from," praised Maggie Cushing. "That Dollie has been at work."

Rev. Temple seated himself while noting the printed agenda Maggie had provided. He was impressed at how organized the meeting had been conducted. He could see that the group had already set up lesson plans along with several other activities for the summer program.

Maggie began speaking and sharing how the ladies had considered a variety of missionaries for the Vacation Bible School, but the other hungry committee members were out of control as they jumped at the chance for another of Dollie's donuts. The meeting temporarily halted.

Linda Morrow opened the refrigerator and brought out the container of milk she had brought and Rachel Parkhurst began pouring coffee for those who wanted it. Sarah Jenkins shared her cookies as did Emily Houseman. Colleen Marx opened her container of fresh squeezed orange juice. It made for a nice break as the ladies relaxed and at the same time reviewed what they had decided.

"What missionary did you choose to support this summer?" asked Rev. Temple as the group continued eating.

"We were thinking we might do something different this year," Maggie Cushing began. "You have preached that we need to get involved in witnessing and helping people in the community. After some discussion we came up with the idea of using the offering to purchase things needed to do various projects for the elderly in the community."

"That's a bit different," commented Rev. Temple. "Go on."

"We complain about some of the yards not being mown here in town. We also talk about the houses that look run down and that need to be painted," commented Emily Houseman. "It seems like these are projects we could easily involve the young people and use it as a witness to the community that we seek to serve Christ."

"I like it," exclaimed Rev. Temple.

"We did a quick survey and most of these houses and yards we are commenting about are owned by people in their 80's or in some cases are a family whose husband is serving in the military overseas," continued Emily Houseman. "Surely we can stop complaining and start doing things to help them."

"I like it!" exclaimed Rev. Temple again.

"So do we!" remarked Maggie Cushing. "The more we thought about it the more we wanted to go out and get started today."

"Let me suggest one thing," said Rev. Temple. "Might be best if you approach them first and say it is a church and community project. Get permission and set up a time to do the work and not just show up and begin. These people do have pride. They can't help that they don't have money to pay someone to do the work. Most are living on a fixed income that barely covers food and basic utilities. You need to tread lightly and work with them."

"Yes," added Colleen Marx. "I remember wanting to have my neighbor's yard cleaned up. I finally did it for her one day and she was so mad at me. She yelled at me about making fun of her and making her feel cheap and useless. I didn't mean to do that. I really meant to do a good deed. Rev. Temple is right. We need to make arrangements with them first."

"Here is another idea that would enable us to get more of the congregation involved," interrupted Sherrie Bennett. "How about we also prepare plates of cookies or treats and take to all the elderly in the neighborhood?"

"I like it!" exclaimed Rev. Temple once again. "You are really focused on doing good today. I love it."

The group continued to discuss various ideas of how to better witness to the community as well as assist people in meeting their needs. The group became more excited as they set in motion the plan to reach into the community with Christian Love.

Each committee member present took on the task of heading an individual committee to do one aspect of the project. Emily Houseman volunteered to prepare a list of those who needed some assistance in getting yards cleaned and houses painted. Colleen Marx volunteered to contact various businesses to get donations to go along with the VBS offering that would enable the young people to start right away on the project. Maggie Cushing took on the task of preparing VBS devotions and lessons to present the plan to the young people. Rev. Temple suggested and volunteered to have a prayer group that would pray for guidance in working together with the people they were going to help. Sarah Jenkins volunteered to oversee the preparing of plates of goodies and to make a list of those who should get them. Lori Calder volunteered to organize the young people into small groups and match them with the various projects.

"This has been a very fruitful meeting," commented Maggie Cushing. "I thank all of you for coming and look forward to working together on this exciting new program. Thanks for coming and if nothing further I adjourn the meeting until next Wednesday morning at 10 a.m."

The group gathered their things and started for the door as one by one they all reached over to pick up one more donut to take with them. Rev. Temple nodded approvingly and said Dollie would be pleased.

CHAPTER THREE

Rev. Temple made a quick trip three blocks away to Roselee's Pizza Place to pick up the pizza he had ordered toward the end of the VBS meeting. He got back just in time to greet Roger Brown as he rolled into the office. The two of them said a prayer of thanks and quickly began eating the delicious smelling Roselee's Special Super Supreme Pizza.

Roselee's Pizza Place was the talk of the town when it first opened. Roselee had been the cook at the local school for 20 years. She had always provided top quality meals even when times were tough. She added a salad bar, a potato bar, and convinced the board to provide breakfast for students in the morning. The result was students who were more alert and able to achieve higher scores on tests. The pizza in her tradition of wanting the meal to be the best it could be contained more toppings, more cheese, tender crust, and an incredible taste.

"Eating this pizza is about as close as you get to heaven here on earth," laughed Rev. Temple.

"Wow!" commented Roger Brown. "This is awesome. This is my first time to taste Roselee's pizza. It certainly won't be my last."

The two ate pizza as the computer warmed up. Rev. Temple started typing his password and soon called up the email page. The dial up was very slow but at least those living in Sassafras Springs could get the internet in this small community. With Roselee's Pizza in hand the wait didn't seem nearly as long as it usually did for the primitive method of getting online.

"How much experience have you had with computers?" asked Rev. Temple.

"Been using them since high school and got advanced training when I entered the military. My tour of duty in Iraq the first time allowed me to use the ability in preparing maps displaying where the enemy was located," stated Roger Brown. "Only recently did I get online to chat. In the military they encouraged you to keep on business as the enemy could sometimes track your position by the use of computer signals."

"First tour of duty," said Rev. Temple with a raised eyebrow. "I didn't realize you had been in the military."

"Yes," remarked Roger Brown," I have done three tours of duty in Iraq. I was in a special unit of rangers that would be called in a few minutes without warning and we would find ourselves on our way to some hot spot in the world in less than an hour."

"You're kidding," said Rev. Temple with a slice of pizza midway to his mouth. "I had no idea. You never said anything."

"Of course I didn't," said Roger Brown. "Our safety depended on secrecy."

"Then you are in a wheelchair due to a war injury? Is that what happened?" asked Rev. Temple.

"No," laughed Roger Brown. "I slipped on a piece of soap in the shower in Kuwait and broke my hip joint in a thousand pieces. Strangest thing too as I had just finished the 3rd tour of duty there and was headed home without a scratch. I couldn't believe a piece of soap did me in when I had been close enough to enemy fire to have holes in my clothes."

Rev. Temple's eyes widened at the thought of holes in Roger's clothes. He looked at Roger a little closer and studied his movements. This man who he had only noticed sitting alone in a corner pew had a remarkable past and few if any in the congregation knew anything about it. Here was a veteran who probably had stories that would classify him as a war hero. Rev. Temple wondered what else Roger had done that he didn't know about.

"Do they deliver?" asked Roger Brown.

"What?" said Rev. Temple as he focused on the computer screen.

"Does Roselee's deliver? I would enjoy having this often but it isn't easy for me to get around town in a wheelchair. It would be nice if they delivered."

"I don't know," replied Rev. Temple. "If they don't deliver, whenever you want one call me and I'll make sure you get one. Ok?"

"Deal," laughed Roger Brown.

"Here's one!" exclaimed Rev. Temple as the emails came on the screen. "Let me click to print the letter."

Roger moved closer to the screen as Rev. Temple printed a copy of the first scam they had located among his emails. Roger quickly spotted other emails and was surprised at how many and how easy they were to find.

"I can't believe there are this many," commented Roger Brown. "I was convinced that I was the only one that got this email about the inheritance in Nigeria. I am beginning to think there were probably hundreds or maybe thousands who received it."

"Exactly," replied Rev. Temple. "That is why I wanted you to come to take a look at these I get. I knew you would understand better if you saw how the people set you up to get your money."

Rev. Temple handed Roger the copy of the first email he had printed. Roger immediately began reading it aloud.

- -

MICROSOFT CORPORATIONS SWEETSTAKES PROMOTIONS: Customer Services

Your Batch No. 2009/281/MCS Your reference number: LUM/L 193/2810

OFFICIAL WINNING NOTIFICATION:

We are pleased to inform you of the release of the long awaited results of the Sweepstakes promotion organized by Microsoft Corporations, in conjunction with the foundation for the promotion of software products, (F.P.S.) held this August, 2009, in the Netherlands. Wherein your email address emerged as one of the online winning emails in the 2nd category and therefore attracted a cash award of 450,000.00 euro (four hundred and fifty thousand euros only) and a Toshiba laptop. To begin your claim, do file for the release of your winning by contacting our Foreign Transfer Manager, Mr. Flip Hubert. Telephone 0031-684-088-467; Fax 0031-847-300-758. Email: microphome.flipzone@googlemail.com.

Microsoft Internet E-Mail Contest Awards is sponsored by former CEO/ chairman Bill Gates and a consortium of software promotion companies: The Intel Group, Toshiba, Dell Computers and other International Companies. Microword Internet Email Contest is held periodically and is organized to encourage the use of the Internet and promote computer literacy worldwide.

Congratulations!!! Sincerely, Mrs. Serena Henrik, promotions director.

- -

"That sounds pretty official to me," stated Roger Brown. "How can you know that it is a scam? I see you own a Toshiba laptop and have a Microsoft program. It seems like you would be a prime candidate to be a winner of the contest. How can you tell this isn't real?"

Rev. Temple scratched his head as he began. "It does seem rather authentic. That is the whole idea. They will use a well known company or something you have seen or heard and use it to get your confidence. I have gotten similar emails claiming to be from the director of the FBI. One was from Ed McMahan and Publishers Clearing House. The only difference was that instead of Publishers Clearing House it was listed as Publishers Clearing Press. The name is very close but is slightly different signaling that it is a scam. Another email used the title Magazine Clearing House. Here I see it is using Microsoft to begin with but suddenly switches to 'Microword.'"

Rev. Temple explained how criminals display things in a professional way using the logo, names of people connected with the company and in some cases the official letterhead that they obtain off the internet. The scammer knows that the name of a company that a person feels comfortable with will cause a person to become more receptive to what is offered.

Rev. Temple continued to explain how he had contacted different companies whose names had been used by scammers. He showed Roger actual letters and emails from the companies denying any connection with the scam email. He explained that the company would quickly release announcements warning of dangers in dealing with the group that had sent the email and state that they were not responsible for the contest or scam being used.

"There are some scams out there that look like they are from Yahoo and they try to get your credit card numbers and a list of personal information," Rev. Temple continued. "Beware of even your local bank. These criminals can duplicate the whole format of the bank statements and fake a letter on their letterhead. The technology we have these days is remarkable but it all provides ways for the criminals to take advantage of people."

"That's incredible!!" said Roger Brown as he continued to shake his head as he learned more about the internet scammers.

"My first question on this one was, 'Why in Amsterdam?'" Rev. Temple continued.

Rev. Temple went on to explain that when a large monetary amount is involved it would probably be handled by phone or in a special overnight delivery or in person. He noted that the winning amount was a huge sum of money. A prize with that much involved would be handled carefully. He noted that a situation with this much money would require the winner to sign a form stating the money had been delivered.

"This was too general and informal to have been real," Rev. Temple concluded. "Let's take a look at another one? This was an example of a fake advertising contest. Another question I had right from the start was 'How did I qualify for this contest when I did not buy a ticket?' Of course you were right about my having a Toshiba laptop and using Microsoft materials. It could be that every purchase was an immediate entry."

"Afraid I would have been trying to get the money," laughed Roger Brown. "I still don't see how you can tell the difference."

"If I sent the personal information that the Foreign Transfer Manager wanted I would quickly have found out. Identity theft would have happened immediately and my account would have lost money or the scammers would have gone the other route of asking me to pay for the delivery of a package with the money in it. Now what company is going to send that kind of money in a box? Either way it smells scam because you don't give out information and you don't pay. Keep that as a rule, Roger."

"Ok," said Roger Brown shaking his head in confusion. "Ah, don't pay to have the money delivered and no secrecy."

"Yes," replied Rev. Temple. "I think you have it. Let's take a look at another."

- -

Attention: Sir/ Madam,

This is to notify you that it has come to our notice that why your funds has not yet being directed to you, both funds held in the World Bank, the CBN, Bank of America or the HSBC Bank. We are therefore directed to inform you that you have not fulfilled your financial obligations and also you have not contacted the legitimate Office for the release of you funds.

Also note that this funds can only be transferred to you through an ATM card, so therefore you are advised to contact Dr. Paul Mike of the International Credit Settlement Department and Also be advised that this transaction will cost you a total fee of $296, this fee is for the procurement of your approval slip. Kindly forward your personal information to Dr. Paul Mike.

If you do not contact Dr. Paul Mike within 7 working days of this notification, your Funds would be revoked. Beneficiaries are advised to keep their Funds details/information from the public to avoid fraudulent claim (IMPORTANT) pending the transfer/claim by Beneficiary.

Congratulations once again!

This is Dr. Paul Mike Contact Information; Ministry of Finance, ATM CARD CENTER, Dr. Paul Mike, <u>atmconsultant_in200@live.com</u>, +234-703-231-2120.

This is the Final Notice from FBI. Robert Muller III.

- -

"Speaking of using FBI Director Robert Mueller, here is one. They misspelled his name but this is how they use his name to give credence to their scam."

"I see," responded Roger Brown. "I would have questioned that for a number of reasons. It says you have a bank account with these various banks. I would think most people would see that couldn't be theirs."

"No," replied Rev. Temple, "all a lot of people see is MONEY. They don't think to reason whether it is really theirs or if it is reasonable. They just see this possibility of money coming their way and jump at it."

"Playing with greed," snapped Roger Brown. "That's all it is—trying to trap us in our own weakness of greed. I see it now."

"There are also a lot of grammatical errors in this one which signals they are overseas and thus not connected with what they are talking about."

"I see."

"Here is a different type," said Rev. Temple pointing to the computer screen. "This will show you the variety of these scams on the internet."

- -

Good day!!!

I have been waiting for you since to contact me for your Confirmable Bank Draft of $1.5 million United States Dollars, but I did not hear from you since for a couple of weeks now. Then I went to the bank to confirm if the draft has expired or getting near to expire and Dr. Wilson the Director Bank of Africa told me that before the draft will get to your hand that it will expire. So I told him to cash the $1.5 USD UNITED STATES DOLLARS to cash payment to avoid losing this fund under expiration as I will be out of the country for a 3 Months Course and I will not come back till ending of November 2009.

What you have to do now is to contact FedEx COURIER SERVICES as soon as possible to know when they will deliver your Consignment to you because of confiscation. For your information, I have paid for the delivering Charge.

The only money you will send to the FedEx COURIER SERVICES to deliver your Consignment direct to your postal Address in your country is ($205.00 US) Two Hundred & Five United States Dollars being their Security Keeping Fee so far. Again don't be deceived by anybody to pay any other money except $205.00 US Dollars. I would have paid that but they said no because they don't know when you will contact them and in case of demurrage.

You have to contact FedEx COURIER SERVICES now for the delivery of your Draft with this information bellow;

Directors Name: Dr. SAM AIL
FedEx COURIER SERVICES
Email Address: (fedexexpress229@live.fr)
Tel/FAX: +229 97-932-215

Finally, make sure that you reconfirm your Postal address and Direct telephone number to them again to avoid any mistake on the Delivery and ask them to give you the tracking number to enable you track your package and know when it will get to your address. Let me repeat again, try to contact them as soon as you receive this mail to avoid any further delay and remember to pay them their Security Keeping fee of $205.00 US Dollars for their immediate delivery.

Note this. The FedEx COURIER SERVICES don't know the contents of the Box. I registered it as a Box of Africa cloths. They did not know the contents were money. This is to avoid them delaying with the BOX. Don't let them know that box contend money ok.

I am waiting for your urgent response.
Yours Faithfully,
Sir O. Odinga

- -

"I can see this one is probably not real," began Roger Brown. "The language in it is questionable."

"On the other hand," suggested Rev. Temple, "it could be as a result of them not speaking English as a first language. The real thing that I see is they ask for money. I delete those immediately. No contest I have ever seen that was authentic was going to ask for you to pay to have the money delivered. In this case we never know why the money is coming. They are just making an arrangement to send it to me."

"Yeah, that doesn't really make sense," responded Roger Brown.

"The secrecy matter is another tip off. Sends a red flag for me every time," added Rev. Temple. "Immediately I question any group that says I have to keep something quiet or can't tell anyone about it until I get the money. Again, there is no authentic contest that will do that as a matter of openness and making sure everything is legal is a part of holding contests. One other thing, sending money in a box marked 'African clothes' is very strange."

"Is that another one," asked Roger Brown as he pointed to the screen.

- -

EUROPEAN GMBH LOTTERY, 40 Avenue de la Toison d, Brussels, Belgium

WINNING NOTICE: We happily announce to you the International Email Address Draw of the European GMBH Lottery held on 25th of August in Brussels, Belgium, your email address have just won you the sum of Eight Hundred Thousand Pounds.

Please note that the lucky winning number falls within our Asia booklet representative in Sarawak, Malaysia as indicated in your play coupon. In view of this, your Eight Hundred Thousand Pounds in cheque would be released to you by our fiduciary agent in Sarawak, Malaysia.

Your email address was attached to Reference Number: G/G/ L312064-3DE980.

To claim your winning prize you are to contact the appointed agent and provide him with these informations:

1. Full name:
2. Address:
3. Occupations:
4. Sex:
5. Country of Residence:
6. Telephone Number:

7. Cell:

Contacts of Claims Agent: Mr. Mohd. Azizan B. Mustaffa (Tele: +60102977483)

302 Jalan Sekama, 96100 Kuching, Sarawak, Malaysia

Sincerely, Mrs. Patricia Banzer, zonal coordinator, European GMBH Lottery.

- -

"I think I'm beginning to see," commented Roger Brown. "These are not very professional often times. They use improper grammar and are located in countries that surprise me. Why would the headquarters be in Malaysia if sponsored in Belgium or some place in Europe?"

"Good question, Roger," responded Rev. Temple. "My guess is there is less chance to catch the people in Malaysia. The rules over contests and lotteries are less watched in the Far East and this spreads the area to cover to catch these people. It is almost impossible to catch them online anyway. Spreading the operation to two continents makes it much more difficult."

"Good point," noted Roger Brown.

"Seen enough?" asked Rev. Temple, "Or do you want to see more?"

"You have more?" said Roger Brown amazed at how easy it was for Rev. Temple to provide examples. "These all came today on your computer? Just how many do you get?"

"Way too many," laughed Rev. Temple. "I probably get a dozen a day."

"Wow!"

"Now let me see," hesitated Rev. Temple as he thought about the various scams. "We had one that was linked to a big company we trust; another was a lottery; and the other was a big sum of money heading your way for no apparent reason. Ah, here is a different kind. This is closer to what you received."

- -

Hello:

How are you and your family? Hope you all are doing alright. My name is Sgt. Christopher Lewis and I am an American soldier serving in the military of the 3rd Infantry Division in Iraq. As you know, we are being attacked by insurgents everyday and car bombings.

I have summed up courage to contact you with a very desperate need for assistance. I found your contact particulars in an address journal. I am seeking your kind assistance to move the sum of Eight Million U.S. Dollars to you as far as I can be assured that my share will be safe in your care until I complete my service here.

Some money in various currencies was discovered in barrels at a farm house near one of Saddam's old palaces in Baghdad, Iraq. During a rescue operation and it was agreed by Staff Sgt. Kenneth Buff and I that some part of this money be shared among both of us before informing anybody about it since both of us saw the money first. This was quite an illegal thing to do, but I tell you what? No compensation can make up for the risk we have taken with our lives in this hell hole. Of which my brother in law was killed by a road side bomb last time. You can read how we discover this money through the link: http://news.bbc.co.uk/2/h/middle_east /2988455.stm.

The above figure was given to me as my share and to conceal this kind of money became a problem for me. So with the help of a British contact working here and his office enjoy some immunity, I was able to get the package out to a safe location entirely out of troubles spot. He does not know the real contents of the package and believes that it belongs to a British-American medical doctor who died in a raid here in Iraq and before giving up entrusted me to hand over the package to his family in the United States. I have now found a very secure way of getting the package out of Iraq to your country for you to pick up and I will discuss this with you when I am sure that you are willing to assist me, and I believe that my money will be well secured in your hand because you have fear of God.

I want you to tell me how much you will take from this money for the assistance you will give to me. One passionate appeal I will make to you is not to discuss this matter with anybody, should you have reasons to reject this offer, please and please destroy this message as any leakage of this information will be too bad for us soldiers here in Iraq. I do not know how long we will remain here and I have been shot, wounded and survived two suicide bomb attacks by the special grace of God. This and other reasons I will mention later has prompted me to reach out for help. I honestly want this matter to be resolved immediately. Please contact me as soon as possible with my email address which is my only way of communication. Please do not bother for anything because I will take care of whatever that required.

God bless you and your family, Sgt. Christopher Lewis.

- -

The two men sat in silence for a moment reading the message. They looked at each other and then back at the letter.

"What do you think?" began Roger Brown.

"I don't know," replied Rev. Temple. "I doubt seriously it is authentic. Too many things involved for it to be real. I don't like the fact he is calling on us to break the law and in the same breath talking about the Grace of God."

"That struck me too," said Roger Brown weakly. "I have been there and know the stress a soldier is under. I can see someone do this and it is true that we would find huge amounts of money around Baghdad. It was tempting to take some as you get the idea that they owe it to you for risking your life. Yet, he says too much."

31

"What do you mean?"

"Something bothers me about it."

"Is there a way to check to see if there is a Sgt. Lewis in the 3rd Division?"

"Sure," said Roger Brown excited to be able to use his training. "Move over and let me at the computer."

In a matter of seconds Roger had called up a list and they were checking it. There was a Sgt. Lewis in the 3rd Division but that division had not been in Iraq for some time. They concluded that if he was the person writing he could not have found the money in Iraq and certainly was not in Iraq now.

"So, what do you think?" asked Rev. Temple.

"Rather a wicked mind to use the emotional things he talks about in this letter to get a person to send money and I can see that is what he intends here. He didn't mention it yet, but he will explain the need for money to be paid to get the money. You can bet on that from what I have seen already in the other scams," said Roger Brown as he began to understand the evil minds at work on the internet. "How could someone do that? Work on the tenderness of people to get money?"

"You have to remember these people are not worrying about anything other than hitting the person where they will most likely respond. He aimed at their greed and from that was able to get their attention," frowned Rev. Temple as he made a mental note to use that as a sermon topic in the near future.

"Not necessarily," responded Roger Brown. "I did not think about the matter of breaking the law as I read the letter. I was moved with compassion because he was risking his life, had been injured several times, and for sure had lost buddies in the bombings. But wait! None of this really happened . . . . at least not like he said. He is not there. There is no money. There is no package making its way to the United States."

"And he wants us to break the law with him," sighed Rev. Temple.

"Exactly!" said Roger Brown raising his voice as he spoke. "The man is not deserving of our concern. This is not a man in Iraq, probably not a soldier, certainly not going to benefit us in anyway. He is basically the scum off the bottom of a box setting on the pond bank after several rains."

"Wow!" laughed Rev. Temple with his eyes wide open at the surprising anger and unique description from Roger. "I do believe you want to meet this man and have some words with him."

"Words?" laughed Roger Brown. "Just let me at him. I'll show him who deserves our sympathy!"

"Maybe we better look at another one to get your mind off of him," said Rev. Temple as he pointed to another he had found. "Here is another based on the same type scam. Let's see how it differs."

- -

Dear Friend,

My name is Elbert Douglas Burnett (Sarge). I am an American soldier serving in the military with the 3rd Army infantry division here in Iraq. I am in a desperate need of your urgent assistance. I have summed up courage to contact you towards assisting me on my quest. I found your particular email in the international email list directory from the Internet here in Iraq and decided to contact you to assist me in moving the sum of $25 million U.S. Dollars (Twenty Five Million United States Dollars) to you in your country of origin or any location of your choice. But I need to be assured that my share will be kept safe in your care until I complete my service here in Iraq.

Some money in various currencies were delivered in barrels at a farm house near one of Late Saddam Hussein's old palaces here in Tikrit-Iraq, during a rescue operation. It was agreed by Staff Sargent Joey Jones and myself and some other officers that part of this money be shared among us before informing anybody about it and turning it over to the troop, since we were the first to discover this money. Though this was quite an illegal thing to do as an army officer, but I tell you what? No compensation can make up for the risk we have taken with our lives in this hell hole of which my brother-in-law was killed by a road side bomb last time and many other American soldiers.

The above figure was given to me as my share and to conceal this find of money became a problem for me, so with the help of a red cross officer working here in Iraq whose office enjoy some immunity, I was able to get the package out to a safe location entirely out of trouble spot as a personal affect of my late brother-in-law. The red cross officer does not know the real content of the package and believes that it belongs to my brother-in-law who died by a road side bomb blast here in Iraq and before giving up, entrusted me to hand over the package to his family in the United States.

I have now found a very safe and secure way of getting the package out of Iraq through Jordan so you can pick it up anywhere and I will discuss this with you when I am sure that you are willing to assist me. I believe that my money will be well secured in your hand because I feel you have the fear of God at heart and that you can be trusted. I intend to part away with 40% of this money as your share for assisting me in concluding this project if we eventually come to a reasonable agreement. You should also assure me that this issue will not be discussed with any other person and will be kept as top secret. Should you have any reason to reject this offer, please and please delete this message for any leakage of this information will be too bad for us soldiers here in Iraq. I am not certain how long it will take before I am discharged from here in Iraq. I have been shot twice, wounded and survived two suicide bomb attacks by the grace of God. This and other reasons earlier mentioned has prompted me to reach out for help by contacting you. I honestly want this issue resolved immediately. Please contact me as soon as possible.

Best Regards,

Elbert Douglas Burnett (Sarge)

- -

"It is the same exact letter. All the same information but a different sergeant's name," said Roger with shock.

"That proves the other is a scam I guess," noted Rev. Temple. "Can you believe it?"

"This one also had a lot of grammatical errors," said Roger Brown as he pointed to a few words placed incorrectly.

"Here is another," said Rev. Temple as he moved on to another example. "All of these have come to my address today. You would think they would know that all these things are going to the same address. They surely don't think there is anyone dumb enough to send money to all of these emails."

- -

LUCKY WINNER: This is to inform you that you were selected for a cash prize of One Million Pound Sterling, UK, held on August, 2009 in London, United Kingdom. Claims Agent Mr. Caly Darien (Tele. +44-704-570-6914) Email: mr.calydarien5@msn.com.

Fill the blanks below:

1. Names:
2. Address:
3. Nationality:
4. Age:
5. Occupation:
6. Sex:
7. Telephone & Fax:

- -

"Rather simple and to the point," laughed Roger.

"Undoubtedly a request for payment to deliver the money comes next after you have given them vital information. Not good. And here is another with a slightly different approach. Says I will have to pay the payment back I received if I don't report to the Nigerian Government the situation with this 20 million dollars," said Rev. Temple.

"You got $20,000,000?" said a shocked Roger Brown.

"No!" responded Rev. Temple. "Of course I didn't. That's part of the scam. They put you in a position that you think you have to turn your bank number over to them to get things settled. Read it closely. You'll see what I mean."

- -

From the Desk of Mr. Sunny Mark
Chairman Contract Verification/Review
Panel and Foreign Debt Payment

Attention: Beneficiary

The Federal Government of Nigeria has been seriously warned by the United States Government, International Monetary Fund (IMF), World Bank, United Nations (UN) and other international bodies to make sure we settle most of our outstanding foreign debts we owed to Next of Kin's, Fund Beneficiaries and foreign contractors that executed contract with us.

In light of this, this present administration under the auspices of the new Civilian Head of State Alhaji Umaru Musa Yar'Adua the President and Commander in Chief of Armed Forces Federal Republic of Nigeria within Five days on assumption of office set up this panel to review, verify and to settle all outstanding legitimate foreign debts the Federal Government of Nigeria owed to next of kin's and foreign contractors that executed contract with the Federal Government of Nigeria for the past five years.

But a very surprising record was discovered in your payment file that is why you have not been contacted about this since then. Records showed that your inheritance payment has been approved four times and duly completed two times. Also we found out that these funds totaling $20.000.000.00 (Twenty Million United States Dollars) was transferred directly from the central bank of Nigeria to the below stated bank account on your authorization. This has now resulted in bringing the USA and British Government into the case and we really want you to explain to us what you know about this transfer/payment

BANK NAME: STANDARD CHATTERED BANK,

BANK ADDRESS, 138-141 1ST FLOOR, EDINBURGH TOWER,

THE LANDMARK, 15 QUEENS ROAD, CENTRAL HONG KONG,

ACCOUNT NAME: INDO-CHINA GROUP LTD,

A/C #: USD114-102-5567-8,

SWIFT CODE: SCBL 11K111

The most baffling part is that your payment keeps coming up in every period of debt reconciliation and verification always receives approval like now.

NOW OUR QUESTION IS, HAVE YOU RECEIVED YOUR FULL PAYMENT OR ANY PART OF YOUR FUND ENTITLEMENT OWED TO YOU BY THE NIGERIAN GOVERNMENT? WE NEED THESE ANSWERS FROM YOU WITHIN 24 HOURS FROM NOW. AND IF WE DO NOT HEAR FROM YOU IMMEDIATELY YOU RECEIVE THIS MESSAGE TODAY, WE WILL ASSUME YOU ARE INVOLVED AND HAVE RECEIVED OVER PAYMENT, WHICH ONE SHOULD BE RETURNED TO NIGERIA

Help us to help you, If not call me immediately you receive this message today on my direct number or send me a details email disclaiming the information so that you will be issued with claim identification code (CIC) which will help you to secure your claim and payment from fraudulent officials. And also you will be advised and guided accordingly on how you will receive your legitimate fund entitlement from the Nigerian Government, which will be credited into your nominated bank account within 72 hours from now.

And you will be required to send us the below stated information for confirmation and record purposes.

1. Your Full Name:
2. Your Direct Telephone
3. Fax Number
4. Your Residential Address:
5. Your Current Receiving Banking Details
    Thanks for your anticipated cooperation.
    Yours truly,
    Mr. Sunny Mark
    The Chairman of Contract Verification/Review
    Panel and Foreign Debt Payment

"They don't miss an opportunity do they," laughed Roger Brown.

"No," laughed Rev. Temple. "These criminals will take advantage of any bad situation that comes along. It is much like the young boy who stands at the corner asking for money for the Jerry Lewis Telethon and then goes with the money and buys drugs or maybe a stick of gum. It is the same principle. Starting with something small and easy their effort and techniques grow into scams like this. They have the brains to have a good normal life but are hooked into the idea of earning money with a smile, clever words and making people feel guilty if they don't respond."

"It is really sad."

"Yes, it is Roger," nodded Rev. Temple. "People are very giving in this country but they are going to stop helping people if they get the idea that all their contributions are going to people who have no desire to help anyone but themselves."

"Oh my!" shouted Roger Brown. "It is 8:30 already. I have to get on my way."

"Hot date?" asked Rev. Temple. "Sorry, guess that wasn't very nice of me to nose into your private life. It has been good to chat with you Roger. Come back soon as I have a lot of things I want to talk over with you."

"Sure thing, Rev." said Roger as he quickly exited the door of the minister's study leaving Rev. Temple alone.

"Here is another one," began Rev. Temple as he looked back at the computer.

CHAPTER FOUR

A few minutes later Roger poked his head in the door and said, "Did you say another one? You sound like this one is unusual."

Rev. Temple jumped with fright at the surprise appearance of Roger in the office again. They laughed as Rev. Temple brought up the email.

"Yes it is," began Rev. Temple. "There are pictures with this one. That is unusual. Here, take a look—and weren't you going home or somewhere?"

"I had not gotten a block and my cell phone rang with information that the meeting had been cancelled. Remembering you saying there was another type of scam email I found myself wanting to come back. I hope you don't mind. My curiosity took over. I had to see if there—well, I couldn't resist seeing what it was."

Rev. Temple and Roger Brown continued looking at the computer for another half hour as they examined the email that included a couple of pictures. One of the pictures was of a man standing in front of a castle. Roger studied the picture closely. Then he looked at the boy.

"I think I know this man," said Roger. "Who is he?"

"I don't have a clue," remarked Rev. Temple. "You saw it just as I saw it. I have not responded to any of these scams."

Looking further in the email they found that the message was from a handsome 22 year old named Lance that claimed he had been a slave in Colorado Springs. His picture showed him to be living in a nice apartment or condo with a deck that displayed an incredibly beautiful view of the mountains. Rev. Temple laughed at the idea that this boy was a slave with the obviously expensive surroundings.

"Slave indeed," laughed Roger Brown. "Who does he think he is fooling?"

"Actually Roger," interrupted Rev. Temple, "I've heard there are a lot of slaves in the United States. I was doing research for a paper last year in a class at college. I was stunned at the stories I found."

"Oh, come on," laughed Roger," you can't be serious?"

"I am afraid I'm not. There are thousands of young people who run away from home and they get caught in the city without a job, no money and are taken in by these pimps or some such people who force them to work on the streets offering sex for money."

"In the United States this happens?" asked Roger Brown.

"Yes," answered Rev. Temple.

"I have seen it in Malaysia and some of the Asian countries, but not here. This is America for goodness sake. Land of the free, home of the brave . . . . well you get the idea."

"Sure," continued Rev. Temple. "You are right. It is a shock to find that there are thousands of young people being sold for sex on the streets and houses in major cities across the country."

"But, well," stuttered Roger Brown. "Why aren't we doing something to rescue them? These young people need to be helped."

"True," said Rev. Temple. "What would you do? How would you go about helping them?"

"The police," suggested Roger Brown. "They should be called and told what is going on."

"Sounds like a good idea but what if they are part of the problem," asked Rev. Temple.

"Wait," sighed Roger. "I'm getting really sick inside. I guess you are saying the problem is too big for us to do anything about?"

"No," said Rev. Temple quickly. "I don't mean to say it is hopeless and that we shouldn't do something about it but we have so many problems right here to deal with."

"This has been quite a day," summarized Roger. "First it was scams and now sex slavery. What is this country coming to? I fear the end of time is just around the corner. God is not going to want to watch this and just like he did in the time of Noah will want to clear the world of this kind of filth."

"Very good point," responded Rev. Temple, "and we need to be trying to help people one at a time as we come in contact with them around us."

"Just like you helping me to understand how I was being taken by these scammers," replied Roger. "Thanks. I am so thankful that you were able to persuade me not to send the money. I honestly would have been in very sad shape financially if I had sent that $10,000."

The two of them returned to the final letter they had pulled up on the screen. In the letter, the boy called the man standing in front of the castle "Dad" and made comment he had no idea where his parents were as he had been taken from them a number of years ago. Roger thought again and strained to think where he had seen the father.

"You really think you know this man?" asked Rev. Temple.

"Yes I do," replied Roger Brown. "Somewhere I have known him or helped him possibly while in the military. I'm not sure."

"Say, since you mention the military," began Rev. Temple. "I would like to know more about your experiences."

"No you wouldn't, Jack," avoided Roger." You really don't want to hear what I have been involved with in the wars. When you are standing next to your friends one minute and seeing their heads and body parts floating down the river in a matter of a few seconds . . . ."

"I'm sorry, Roger," apologized Rev. Temple. "I was being insensitive. I am sure you have seen a lot that I can't even imagine."

Roger switched back to the picture of the father and looked closer at the young son to determine if there was any relationship. He flipped back to the letter and studied it with such intensity that Rev. Temple began to think Roger might know more than he was saying.

"You remember anything about this man yet?"

Roger nodded negatively and then requested a copy of the photographs. Rev. Temple clicked on the print control and then got up from his chair and walked toward the computer. There he collected the printed copies of both Lance and the one Lance had called his father. While Rev. Temple was busy, Roger quickly scribbled the screen name and address for Lance that appeared in the letter.

"Honestly, Roger," stated Rev. Temple as he turned to return with the pictures, "these kinds of letters are sent a lot and they are usually college kids sitting in a dorm room making up all of this stuff to get you to send money to them. They will say they are an orphan left on the street or in the hospital after their entire family was killed in a car wreck and that they have no one to help them. The big push is to get money sent for one reason or another. They work hard on your emotions."

"Could I have a copy of this letter?" asked Roger hoping it would get Rev. Temple distracted again. "I'll put it on the wall to remind myself not to get involved with these scammers."

Rev. Temple clicked on print and again went to the printer to collect a copy of the letter. Roger quickly wrote on a piece of paper another email address he noted above the letter. As Rev. Temple turned around Roger pressed the bit of paper in his pocket to keep Rev. Temple from seeing it.

"Guess you are probably hungry and I should be going. It is getting late," Roger said. "Thanks for making the copies of the pictures and the letter. I don't suppose I'll be able to identify them or remember where I might have met this older man. I am probably mistaken, but would like a little time to think. I'll toss them in the trash in a couple of days if I don't come up with any ideas on where I have seen this older man."

The two men said "Good night" to each other and Roger headed home. He quickly entered the house, switched on the computer and typed in the yahoo address he had written down from the email at the church building. In a matter of seconds a young man came online and greeted Roger.

"Hello Sir," began Lance. "I am slave Lance. Who are you Sir?"

"I am Roger and I'm pleased to meet you tonight. I was at a friend's house and saw your email and pictures," typed Roger Brown. "My friend was showing me a variety of scams online when your email came on. When my friend was looking the other way I quickly scribbled the address on a piece of paper. I believe I know your father as I also saw his picture."

"You know my father! Do you know where he is? I would be very much in your debt if you could tell me where he is. I have been looking for him."

Roger paused for a moment still straining to remember where he had known this man in the photograph.

"For some reason I am getting the impression you are not from the USA," questioned Roger. "Is that correct?"

"I was kidnapped while in Argentina," came the quick response from Lance. "Well, not exactly kidnapped. I ran away from my mother and Master Dan found me and said he would bring me to the United States if I would serve him as a slave."

"Slave?" responded Roger. "What does that mean?"

"I do housework and cook."

"So you—oh?" replied Roger surprised at the answer he got. "You work doing housework? Why does that make you a slave?"

"Yes, I didn't want to do all that but it was the only way he would bring me to the United States," added Lance. "I thought I could find my Dad right away but this is a much bigger country than I remember."

"Still how does that make you a slave?" continued Roger Brown.

"He didn't pay me," replied Lance. "I have to do everything he wants and he provides a place for me to live and food."

"I see," puzzled Roger. "You are right about the United States. It is rather big. So where is your Dad?"

"I thought you knew?" responded Lance.

"No, I said I thought I knew your Dad. I'm afraid I don't know where he is at the moment."

"I thought you knew where he was. You probably don't even know him. You are just teasing me," accused Lance. "Sir, I'm in terrible need of food right now and this doesn't help me. I haven't eaten in two days."

"You need food? I thought you had a master. Does he not feed you?"

"Not any more. He was transferred to Hong Kong and I have not seen him in six months."

Roger was spinning with confusion at Lance's comments. He looked back over the comments and studied them for details. He was determined to catch Lance in a lie or something to convince himself that it was a scam.

"He brought you here from Argentina and then dumps you on the street? Now that is some kind of master."

"No, no, no," grumbled Lance. "He actually gave me an apartment for six months."

Roger scooted the chair back at that response. He took another look at the picture of the older man who Lance called his father. Shook his head and typed again.

"I'm confused. So are you on the street homeless or what?" Roger asked.

"I will be at the end of the week. My master paid for six months and it ends this weekend. I'll be on the street. I don't have any money and no food."

"What do you plan to do?" questioned Roger.

"I have been looking for a new master. I don't know what else to do."

"So your mother is in Argentina?" asked Roger

"Yes, that is correct," replied Lance "I ran away because I want to be with my Dad."

"And he is in the United States," added Roger.

"Yes, I told you that Sir. He lives or lived in Ontario, Oregon. I liked it there."

"Ontario? Don't you mean Canada instead of Oregon?"

Roger quickly got the pictorial maps book and glanced at Oregon. He was sure there was no such place and would have Lance on the ropes with questions. Then he spotted Ontario, Oregon. There was such a place. Roger pursued more information as he tried to trip Lance up, but Lance gave plenty of information supporting the idea that he had actually lived there.

"So have you been to England?" asked Roger as he changed the direction of his questions. "This picture of your Dad has a castle. In fact I recognize this castle. I saw it about an hour drive from London when I was there last year."

"Oh I doubt that is in England. I don't think we ever were in England Sir."

"Did you send me an email, Lance?" asked Roger. "I see I have an email from you. What did you send me?"

"Yes, it is a picture of me when Master Dan took me at the first while I was in Argentina," answered Lance.

Roger opened the email and then printed a copy of the picture. It was rather a unique picture. It appeared to be a structure like a bookshelf but there were chairs in the various slots instead of books. In the middle square was Lance holding a sign.

"This was at Master Dan's furniture store. It is a chair display. Each square has a different type of chair except for the center one at the bottom where I am sitting," explained Lance.

"Rather a nice display. Clever actually," complimented Roger. "What is that you are holding? Looks like a sign. What does that say?"

"It just says I love Master Dan, but he is gone now. I have to find another master. Will you be my Master? I'll do all your household work and yard work. I can make you happy. I really need money for food. I haven't eaten in two days and I'm getting sick and weak."

"So you are hungry and have no money. If I recall you are in Colorado Springs?"

"Yes Sir."

"I do have some money here. Too late to get more from the bank, but I do have a little here. I tell you what I will do. I'll send what I have to you. Do you know where the Western Union is located?"

"Oh thank you Sir. That is wonderful of you Sir. Won't you take me as your slave, Sir?"

"Now quit talking about being a slave. I'm a Christian and I'm sending you money to help you out. I don't want you starving," explained Roger.

"Anything you want Sir," continued Lance. "I'll do anything you want if you will take care of me."

"No, no," began Roger. "On the other hand, maybe I could help you find your Dad and help get you straightened out. Perhaps bringing you here would be a good idea."

"How much money are you sending me, Sir. I could sure use it now. I'm very hungry. I have not had food for two days."

"You poor boy," typed Roger. "I'll be right back. The Western Union office is just down the street a block. I'll be right back and then you can go get the money and eat as soon as I give you the confirmation number. Stay here and I'll be right back."

"Thank you, Sir. You are a good Master."

"Hey, now don't talk like that," said a disgusted Roger. "There will be none of that kind of talk. I'm just helping you. Do you understand that?"

"Yes Sir, I'm sorry Sir."

Roger reached for his cookie jar and took out money he had saved away for a rainy day. He thought to himself, "I shouldn't do this, but . . . . I know his Dad. I'm sure of it."

He opened the door and rolled out and down the street to Western Union located at the local Red Basket Grocery Store. There he wired $50 to Lance with the hope that it would provide good meals for a couple of days.

CHAPTER FIVE

"Where have you been?" asked Dollie Burgess, landlord for Rev. Temple. "I thought you would be here tonight for dinner and I made some special things for you."

"Hmmmm!" sounded Rev. Temple as he entered the kitchen. "What is that incredible smell?"

"Food," laughed Dollie Burgess.

Dollie was the best cook around most thought and when she went to work to surprise someone with a delicious hot meal the person better be ready to eat plenty. This was one of those nights and for Rev. Temple to be late was not a good thing. There was Dollie's lasagna and garlic bread waiting to be eaten. Rev. Temple had of course devoured a super supreme pizza from Roselee's with Roger and was still full.

"Dollie," Rev. Temple began as he looked around the kitchen at all the food that had been prepared, "did you think I would eat all of this?"

He looked at the stainless steel 13 inch long pan and saw the lasagna ready to be served. It looked beautiful with sprinkled parmesan cheese and an arrangement of noodles and macaroni on top to form a horn of plenty appearance.

Beside it was a loaf of Dollie's homemade Italian bread toasted with the smell of garlic. There too was a large serving bowl of lettuce, chopped carrots, diced onions, and shredded purple cabbage for a salad. As he ran his eyes down the counter he could see a salad of fruit, a platter of sliced ham, deviled eggs and baked beans.

"You out did yourself," he continued. "This is incredible. There must be enough for a dozen people."

"Right you are," she laughed. "I invited a dozen people over to surprise you. Did you forget it is your birthday?"

Rev. Temple stopped for a minute and looked puzzled. He had forgotten it was his birthday and was even more surprised that Dollie knew. He didn't remember telling anyone about his birthday or when it was. For a number of years he had said he was 21 and holding not wanting to allow himself to get white hair, wrinkles or any of the other aging signs. For him birthdays were just another day.

Dollie handed him a plate and began spooning lasagna on it, but stopped when she saw Rev. Temple's frown.

"Problem?" she began. "You don't like lasagna?"

"Oh, no!" he responded. "I love your lasagna. It is just—well, I ate a super supreme pizza with Roger Brown tonight."

"Roger Brown?" she questioned. "Weren't you with him this morning? What have you two got going these days?"

"He was about to send $10,000 to a total stranger who claimed Roger had won $3 million dollars in some lottery or something."

"He what!" exclaimed Dollie. "Wait until I tell Maggie about this!!!"

"No, no," said Rev. Temple as he reached to stop her motion to the phone. "He didn't win anything. He was about to be scammed. He had received this email online that he had won and to send $10,000 to settle the legal work on his receiving the prize."

"I never heard of such a silly thing," she questioned. "What kind of contest has you pay for the legal matters in receiving the money?"

"Exactly," laughed Rev. Temple. "No contest would. Roger was being taken—for $10,000."

Dollie and Rev. Temple continued to discuss the matter and she nodded that she had enough trouble keeping her bank account without cluttering it up with a million dollars. Rev. Temple explained how Roger was planning to build the new addition to the church and had expressed a desire to include a place for the young people to get together for fun in their spare time.

"I never knew he was that rich," she continued as she spooned lasagna on Rev. Temple's plate.

"He isn't," went on Rev. Temple. "You missed the point. He was going to spend $10,000 to get the money for the church. He really thought he was doing a good thing. Roger doesn't have that kind of money and he would have been in bad financial trouble if he had sent the money. Thankfully Travis Lowry at the bank stopped him in time."

Dollie handed Rev. Temple the plate of lasagna and before Rev. Temple knew it he was shoveling the food into his mouth and enjoying the delicious flavors. Dollie knew just the right ingredients and seasonings. He reached for another piece of garlic bread and mopped the sauce with it and then took a big bite.

"Hmmm," he muttered. "Dollie, you ought to can your sauce and sell it. This is awesome. Even as full as I am I'm still enjoying every bite."

"Full?" Dollie asked. "You can't be full. There is strawberry pie yet."

"Oh dear," groaned Rev. Temple. "I can't possibly eat pie after this. How about I eat it for breakfast? Yes, that would be perfect."

Dollie looked at him and nodded it would be better than making himself sick. She started picking up dishes and clearing the table. She placed Saran Wrap on the leftovers as she placed them in the refrigerator. Rev. Temple could see the strawberry pie and motioned with a thumbs up that it looked very good.

"So Roger was going to risk $10,000 to get the money needed to build the addition to the church," said Dollie as she mulled the matter over in her mind. "I don't really know anything about him. He always sits over on the north side by himself."

"Yes," remarked Rev. Temple. "I'm afraid I don't know much about him either except he is in a wheel chair. I don't even know where he lives. That is awful. Me the preacher too. I'm ashamed."

"I've heard people talk about him," she started.

"Anything I should know?" responded Rev. Temple.

"Not sure," she hesitated. "They say he is a dangerous man. Not heard any particulars about the matter but they seem to think we should keep our children away from him."

"I don't understand," frowned Rev. Temple.

"You know," said Dollie with a look at him like he should understand without her having to say what it meant.

"I still don't know what you mean," laughed Rev. Temple.

"I don't really know anything," she said dropping the conversation.

One more time Dollie asked Rev. Temple to explain the order of events and specifically what Roger had said. Rev. Temple summarized how Roger was going to sacrifice money he needed to obtain money he hoped could be used by the church. Then Rev. Temple expressed that he was going to ask the board to make an effort to get Roger involved in a more vital part of the congregation.

Dollie groaned and got a troubled look on her face as she looked at Rev. Temple. With a nod she asked a few questions and then encouraged Rev. Temple to hold off on the idea. After a bit more discussion they both agreed that the fact he was in a wheel chair had prevented them from asking him to be involved in a variety of projects, but maybe they should get to know more about him before handing over the church building key or some such thing.

"I'm just thankful we were able to stop him from sending the money," said Rev. Temple.

"I am too, but that doesn't explain why you were so late getting home," continued Dollie as she returned to her disappointment in not being able to surprise Rev. Temple with the birthday party. She picked up the last casserole dish of baked beans and placed it in the very crowded refrigerator. Dollie was known for excellent planning and this time she had failed to get the guest of honor to the party. She wanted to examine the situation to make sure that didn't happen again.

"Roger and I met at the office to look at some scams online. I wanted him to see that he wasn't the only one getting them. It helped him to see that it really was a scam. We studied some that were fake lotteries, an emotional letter from a serviceman in need, a fake advertisement contest and some other methods used daily by the criminals."

"Well, that should help him understand not to send money to strangers," she laughed. "I had no idea there were so many crooks online or so many ways they could trick you out of your money. You may need to show me how to recognize them if my son gives me the computer he talked about. He said we could see each other on camera and that way I could see my grandson any time I wanted. I do like the sound of that. But scams? Wow, not sure I'm ready for that."

"Yes, computers are amazing and they help to bring families and friends much closer if taken advantage of properly," said Rev. Temple. "On the other hand, there are people who develop every possible way to use it to rip people off—to get a free meal—to steal from those whose hearts are caring and good."

"Truly sad," commented Dollie.

"Sometimes it isn't the people who are caring and good the crooks are after," Rev. Temple continued. "Sometimes it is the greedy they are looking for who want a fast buck. The crook will dangle a bit of money out there and lure a victim into their trap. It is a disgrace in our country to have people responding because of personal greed to these fake letters. We need to warn people about these vultures."

"How do these scam artists go to bed at night after doing this?" Dollie asked. "Don't they realize they are taking money needed by families? Because of them there are children who probably go to bed hungry. There are couples who fall into financial trouble over something like this and may get divorced. It is a sad thing."

"True," agreed Rev. Temple, "but we know that Roger is at least one less person who will be sending money because of scams and fakes."

Meanwhile across town, Roger unlocked the door to his apartment as he arrived back from Western Union. He clicked his computer on and entered Yahoo Messenger. He typed in the confirmation number for the $50 he had wired to Lance in Colorado Springs. Very quickly a reply was received from Lance thanking Roger for providing money for food.

Lance's name quickly went dark on the yahoo messenger list on Roger's computer. Lance was gone. Roger then wondered if he would ever hear from Lance again as he contemplated what he had just done.

"So was it a scam?" Roger asked himself. "Did I just fall into a trap just minutes after talking with Rev. Temple? I believe I agreed with Rev. Temple not to send money to strangers. Yep, that was the message and here less than an hour later I sent $50 to a total stranger. I'm pathetic."

CHAPTER SIX

On Friday, the ladies met at the church at 7 a.m. They were dressed in old clothes and their hair tied back with large bandannas or bonnets. They had brought rakes, hoes, clippers, baskets and a wheel barrow to start work as soon as they could. They looked well prepared to go out into the world raking leaves, weeding flower beds and painting houses and fences.

"Where is Rev. Jack," asked Maggie. "I assumed he would have donuts from Dollie to share with us."

Shame on you," laughed Joan. "But a donut would be good right now. Did anyone bring coffee?"

"Hey, would someone help me," hollered Colleen Marx. "Ike sent these delicious cinnamon rolls to share with the ladies and I feel sure he meant for us to eat part of them."

"Wow," shouted the ladies as they made a rush toward Colleen.

"Just a minute," Colleen said as she placed the rolls back in her passenger side seat. "Let's unload the back of the truck first."

The ladies crowded around the truck and began removing cans of paint, bags of fertilizer, plants ready to be planted and a lawnmower. They opened a box of cotton gloves and a bag of knee pads. Another box of small garden trowels was removed. Drop cloths, ant stakes, mole traps, and rakes were unloaded.

"Colleen!" said Rev. Temple as he came out of the church office. "Where in the world did you get all of these things? Surely you don't expect us to pay for this?"

"Pay?" laughed Colleen. "Don't you recall I was to contact the businesses to get materials donated and every one of them donated except Sam's Market. Everywhere I went the business owners were excited about our project—that is except for the Market. Sam said I had to fill out some paper to get it approved and then I might get $5. You would think he would donate a lot from the kind of money we spend there."

"I don't believe it. That isn't what I think it is, is it?" continued Rev. Temple looking at the unloaded lawn mower from the back of Colleen's truck. "Who donated it? I used to have one of those when I was in high school. I used one of those to make money to buy my first car."

Rev. Temple turned the machine around to make sure it was the brand he thought it was. "Yes, it is a Swisher Lawn Mower. I thought it had to be. These are great mowers."

"Jake's Repair donated it," Colleen quickly said as she nodded in agreement about the efficient way the mower worked. "Jake Swindell said it was a rebuilt lawn mower he had found at a flea market. After looking it over he thought it would work pretty well with some adjustments and it did. He was certain it would come in handy today."

"This is great," continued Rev. Temple. "I volunteer to use it part of the time. My, the memories it brings back."

Rev. Temple continued to examine the mower as he opened the area where the oil went. He checked to see that the filter was clear and touched the mower blades for sharpness.

"Oh, by the way, Sam can't be expected to donate to every fundraiser," said Rev. Temple. "Remember they did contribute to the choir festival."

"Rev. Temple," hollered Sarah Jenkins from the back door of the church building. "There is a telephone call for you—something about a couple coming here to meet you about getting married."

"Oh, that's right," he said as he turned to the group. "Ladies, I forgot I had an appointment today. I won't be able to go with you. Now remember to always ask before you start working on the people's yards or houses."

"Did you understand him?" Colleen asked.

"Said something about not going with us," laughed Sarah as she joined the group. "What can I do?"

"Here," said Colleen as she handed a cinnamon roll to Sarah. "Eat this."

Sarah took the roll with a laugh and said, "Sure thing!"

The ladies quickly passed the box of cinnamon rolls from Ike's and launched into talking about plans each one had for the day. They discussed who would be better at mowing and who would do a better job weeding flower beds. Some said they would prefer to do painting. Quickly the ladies put together working crews to handle about every possible situation. Then they started thinking of people who might appreciate their assistance. A list of a dozen properties was assembled before one person recommended they drive around the community to find others.

As soon as the cinnamon rolls were gone the ladies loaded the cars to tour the town looking for places to do good deeds. A short distance down the first street, the ladies soon pointed at one particular house. They discussed who lived there and decided they might as well get to work and clean it now. They exited the car with rakes and clippers and charged toward the house as though they were a platoon of the army on operations.

"Hey!" yelled Justin McGorney as he stuck his head out the front door. "What do you people think you are doing? Get off my property."

Mr. McGorney strutted out of his house and on to the lawn with a ball bat in his hand. He looked around and began swinging the bat in all directions.

"Hi, Mr. McGorney," began Emily Houseman as she approached Mr. McGorney and ducked just in time to prevent being hit. "We just came by to help you clean your yard and make it look nice."

"What kind of rip off you ladies pulling," asked a mistrusting Justin McGorney.

"No rip off," laughed Sherrie Bennett. "We just want to show our Christian love for our neighbors by helping clean their yards and painting their houses."

"Do you, now?" said Justin with one eye squinting at them as he examined the group. "I don't know any of you old women."

The ladies stopped what they were doing and turned in unison toward the man who was a good 20 years older than the oldest one of them. They looked at his white beard, his dirty and ripped trousers and yellowed t-shirt. They looked at his worn out tennis shoes. They watched as he limped back on to the front porch hanging on to the railing as he shook a fist at them and told them to get out of his yard.

Rather confused the ladies gathered at the corner of his property and looked at the sad condition of the house and yard. They looked at each other and with a shrug loaded back into the cars and focused on finding another location to share their Christian love.

Mrs. Georgia Maddox lived a block away. When the ladies came to her house they all pointed and motioned to stop the car. They immediately jumped out and marched to the flower beds on the south side of the house. Some of the ladies began working on trimming the roses and weeding her flower beds. Others went to work on fertilizing the yard that was brown and was nearly bare of grass. Another individual started seeding the yard.

Good progress had been made on the south side of the yard by the time a big double cab truck pulled in the driveway. The women were feeling pretty good about the job they had done cleaning the yard and weeding the flowerbeds. They were proud at how everything looked. Some of the women began getting back up on their feet after kneeling to pull weeds and looked to see who was in the truck. They hoped to receive compliments and praise for their demonstration of Christian love after getting such a disappointing response from Mr. McGorney.

The sound of a truck door opening was heard followed by the echoing slam of the same door. Everyone stopped what they were doing and turned toward the truck. There was Mrs. Maddox wearing green coveralls and high top boots. She had a straw hat on top of her head and it was pulled down on the forehead of her angry looking face.

"Women!!" shouted Mrs. Maddox, "Did my daughter send you over here to do this? I'm not going to have my daughter paying to have my yard work done. If I want it done I'll do it myself. So you women just pack up your things and get out of here."

"Excuse me, Georgia," began Emily Houseman, "your daughter doesn't know we are doing this and there is no charge. We are from the Nickerson Church and are intending to help people in the neighborhood clean up their yards and gardens."

"What kind of scam is this?" Georgia went on shouting. "Oh, I know what you are doing. You women will finish the job and then send me a bill. I know your kind. Church charity indeed! You women are wicked with your bazaars and bake sales and now going around taking advantage of old people. You should be ashamed. Go home to your husbands and leave me alone. If you are not gone in one minute I'm calling the police."

The church ladies tried again to explain that they wanted to help Georgia keep her yard looking nice. They insisted there was no charge, no bill, nothing but free labor and then explained how they had decided to use the mission money from the VBS to do work in the local community. They went on to tell about the various local businesses that had donated things and what a wonderful project it was.

"I don't need your help," Georgia insisted. "Now, ladies, who will care to explain what is wrong with my yard? I think it looks pretty nice. What is this 'eye sore' you talk about?'

The ladies looked at each other and scanned the yard where vines had choked out the flowers in the flower beds, unwanted bushes were flourishing in the fence row, and broken limbs lay in the yard. They looked at the peeling paint on the porch railing and noticed the wires on the side of the house were flapping in the breeze.

"I do pretty well, don't I," continued Georgia. "See, there is no need for your interference. Now get out of my yard!"

As the ladies prepared to leave, Sarah Jenkins took Georgia a plate of homemade cookies. The plate looked very nice with a variety of types of cookies. It was covered with Sarah Wrap and a little pink and white bow was centered on the plate.

Georgia thanked the ladies for the plate of cookies and then dumped them in the trash. The ladies gasped and started grumbling among themselves about the rude, disrespectful, ungrateful people in the community.

"So, ladies?" said Georgia. "Do I call the police or are you going now?"

The ladies returned to the church building depressed at their failure to do anything for anyone. Sarah raised a box of cookies and asked what she should do with them. Colleen took the box and placed it on the table.

"Ladies," Colleen called, "dig in! We deserve the cookies. We worked hard and it may be all we get."

The women ate the cookies themselves that they had intended to give to the people as they worked in yards and painted. Each lady voiced their opinion about the day and unanimously agreed that none of the people on their list of those needing assistance deserved to receive a gift of cookies after the way the ladies had been ordered off properties without a single thank you.

"So ladies," began Rev. Temple as he entered the room. "How did your project go today?"

Silence came over the room. Rev. Temple looked around the group and then realized they were eating the cookies intended to go to the people on the list. Colleen picked up the box and motioned for him to have one.

"I don't understand," continued Rev. Temple. "I thought these were for the people on the list. What happened?"

CHAPTER SEVEN

"With this picture of your dad I am guessing your mother must have been from Argentina and he is from England. Am I right?" asked Roger Brown.

"No, I told you he is from Ontario, Oregon," replied Lance. "He is an American."

Roger signed with relief realizing he could have been working with an illegal alien. This proved Lance was an American.

"And how you got in the United States was due to some man from China bringing you here as a slave or something like that," continued Roger. "Is that right?"

"Yes Sir."

"Your father is American and that makes you an American citizen."

"Yes Sir."

"You mentioned you lived in Ontario, Oregon. How did you get there?"

"You don't listen very well. I said that was where my Dad was from Sir."

"You did say that, didn't you?" responded Roger. "Sorry. How did you get with a master?"

"I met my first master in Argentina, Sir."

"Before or after you went to Oregon with your dad?"

"My parents were married when we were living in Ontario, Oregon. We were not exactly happy but we were a family. It was nice for a little while."

Roger smiled. This was the first sign that Lance had a good relationship with his family. Roger thought to himself about the man in the picture again that Lance had said was his father. He was certain that he knew the man, but nothing brought back memories. It was obvious they had both been in the same locations in England. The story of Ontario, Oregon, seemed to be accurate and plausible, but Roger had never been in Oregon and had no relationship with that part of the country.

"So now what," Roger thought. "What do I do?"

"Are you going to have me come live there with you, Sir?"

"I'm guessing your parents divorced and perhaps you were sent to stay with your mom. I don't mean to be asking a lot of questions, but I like you and despite not having money to help you right now I want to help you."

"Would you be my master? I can come be there with you and help you around the house. Would you like that?" asked Lance as he made his case for Roger to send money."

"Actually I could use some help around the house. I'm in a wheel chair. Does that change your mind about coming since I'm in a wheel chair?"

"Of course not. So you could use my help for sure. Would you send money for me to ride the bus to join you?"

Roger stopped and considered the situation. "Lance is not an illegal alien. He is an American citizen. He needs help and it would be a benefit to have him around the house to help me since I'm in a wheelchair. Perhaps this is how God works," thought Roger as he sought to understand the situation he was in.

"You really do need my help as forgetful as you are. My Dad is American. I told you that."

"Where do you think your Dad is now?" asked Roger.

"Dad," thought Lance. "He is either in the United States, England, Kenya, or Argentina."

Roger was not prepared for that lengthy list of possibilities. He understood the United States and up to this point Lance had said he didn't think the family had been in England. This time he included it. Argentina was where the mother came from. Now how does Kenya come in all this?

"My mom got divorced from my dad and they made me go to Argentina. I didn't want to go. She was a mean mother. She only wanted more money in settlement so she worked to try to get custody of me. Had nothing to do with her wanting to take care of me."

"So it must have been a very bad time for you?" sympathized Roger. "How did Kenya get on the list?"

"That was where we were living at the time they divorced," responded Lance.

Roger's head made a thump as he dropped it to the table. He was lost again. He reread all the notes he had written in an effort to understand who Lance was. So they lived in Kenya . . . . not the United States, England or Argentina until the divorce when the mother and Lance went there.

"Yes Master, but I don't want to talk about it. Do you want me to come there or not? I checked and it will cost $99 for a bus ticket and I truly want to join you there."

"So to get away from your mom you went with a Master . . . is that right?"

"Sort of, Sir."

"What does that mean?"

"My mother's family members are rather powerful people but with power comes danger. My life was in danger as long as I was in their house. I ran off to get free of the dangers and the constant threat of the Gestapo."

Roger's head hit the table again. His mind was rolling with amazement at the story unfolding on the computer monitor. He thought to himself. "I am crazy if I speak with this kid again. He has to be totally fabricated by a fraternity group of guys playing online."

"Chester Wilson was my first master," Lance continued. "He was a furniture salesman in Argentina. Soon after I became his slave he brought me to America. Again, I came as a slave hoping to run off as soon as we got here so I could find my father. I soon saw that was not going to be easy and remained as a slave with Mr. Wilson."

"The store you were in is like one I have seen in England with the chair display and of course the picture of your dad included a castle in the background. I have been to England several times and have been to it. In fact your dad continues to look familiar, but then I know thousands of people . . . . Lance, I'm so confused about all of this. Who are you? Really?"

Roger rolled away from the computer and into the bathroom. Reaching into the medicine cabinet he brought out a bottle of Excedrin. He opened it and emptied one tablet in his hand. He looked at it and finally nodded yes. He needed one. He filled a glass of water and took the pill. Lance had given him a first class headache.

"Okay, Sir. Ah? You know thousands of people? Why?"

"I just do," laughed Roger as he began to relax a bit. "No special reason. As for your dad I'm not sure that I know him now. I just don't know. I can't place him."

"You can know him because he was a contractor perhaps," suggested Lance. "That is why we were in Kenya."

Roger rolled his eyes. Getting information out of this boy was difficult but it came slowly and never when expected.

"Would you like me to help you find your Dad?" asked Roger. "No promises that I can, but I would try if you want me to help you."

"No."

"No?" sad a surprised Roger. "You don't' want me to help you find your father? Is that what you are saying? I won't unless you ask me to."

"Sir," interrupted Lance, "yes Sir. Okay. I appreciate that Sir. My birthday is June 24. That is very close and I would like to be there with you by then."

Again Roger rolled his eyes as more information popped out at the most unexpected time. He contemplated the matter of buying Lance a bus ticket and finally decided having him in the same room might be easier than trying to communicate online.

"Ok, I'll send you the $99 to take the bus here. Let me check the schedule."

"Thank you Sir. I love you for this."

"Hey, now don't talk that way. I'm just trying to help you. You are not going to be my slave and you can stop saying 'Sir' every time. And most of all stop talking the 'love' stuff. I don't expect anything in return. I just want to help you."

"Yes Mr. Roger. Thank you very much."

"Mr. Roger? Well, hummm. Ok, I guess that will do."

"So when are you wiring me the money?"

"I'll go do it now. I'll be back in about 45 minutes with the confirmation number. Talk to you then."

"Thank you Mr. Roger. You are a wonderful man."

"Wait, Lance," quickly responded Roger. "According to the schedule you will arrive at the bus station in Kansas City at 6:30 a.m. That can't be true. It takes you 15 hours to get here. I could drive it in less time."

"It makes stops every few miles to pick up other people. I leave on one bus in Colorado Springs and then switch buses in Denver. Then change buses again in some other city in Kansas. I forget where. Colby I think."

"Yes, I see that now. Wow! You think you can make these two bus changes? One layover is 3 hours in the middle of the night."

"Sure Mr. Roger. I have done this before. I can do it."

"You have been to Kansas City before?" questioned Roger.

"No, not Kansas City," replied Lance. "I have traveled buses before and that is how they are."

"Ok, if you say so. Let me see, that means I have to leave here at 4:30 a.m. to be at the bus station to meet you at 6:30," said Roger. "This should be good. Who can I get to take me there at that time of the day?"

"Is there a problem?" asked Lance.

"No, I'll manage. See you tomorrow morning."

"Love you Mr. Roger," said Lance. "Thanks for everything."

"Hey, what did I say about that love stuff? Now cut that out. I'm just helping you out."

"Sorry, Sir."

"Later Lance."

Roger turned his computer off and again tried to think who he could get to take him to Kansas City to the bus terminal. The only name he could think of was Rev. Temple.

"He did help me out," considered Roger, "when he thought I was going to be scammed out of $10,000. On the other hand, he thinks he has persuaded me not to send money to total strangers. What am I going to tell him to get him to take me to Kansas City?"

He wheeled to the Western Union and wired $120 to Lance thinking Lance would need food as well. Afterwards he rolled his wheel chair by the church office. He tapped on the outside office door and was relieved to have it open with Rev. Temple on the inside.

"So, find any more scams on the computers, Rev. Temple?" asked Roger.

"Roger! I was going to come by your place," began Rev. Temple. "By the way, where is your place? I'm embarrassed. I don't even know where you live. It isn't listed in our church directory either."

"Tell you what," laughed Roger. "I'll tell you my address if you will be there at 4:30 tomorrow."

"That seems simple enough," replied Rev. Temple. "So what is happening then?"

"I hate to ask you but I need someone to take me to Kansas City to the bus terminal. I have a friend's son coming in and I don't know anyone else who will take me. Any chance you would help me out?"

"I can do some sermon preparation in the morning and then do some errands on my way over to your place. Should work out fine," planned Rev. Temple. "Here is another scam you might like to see. I just ran across it as you knocked on the door."

"Scam?" laughed Roger nervously. "You aren't still worried about those are you?"

Rev. Temple clicked and brought the newly found scam on the screen.

- -

ATTENTION: Beneficiary

My name is Mrs. Mary Susan Derrick. I am a US Citizen. I am one of those that executed a contract to Nigeria 4 years ago and they refused to pay me. I had paid over $26,000 trying to get my payment all to no avail.

So I decided to travel down to Nigeria with all my compensation documents and I was directed to see Rev. Pato Messi, who is the member of COMPENSATION AWARD COMMITTEE, and I contacted him and he explained everything to me. He said whoever is contacting us through emails are fake.

He took me to the paying bank for the claim of my Compensation payment. Right now I am the most happiest woman on earth because I have received my compensation funs of $1,500,000.00. Moreover, Rev. Pato Messi, showed me the full information of those that are yet to receive their payments and I saw you as one of the beneficiaries, and your email address, that is why I decided to email you to stop dealing with those people. They are not with your fund. They are only making money out of you. I will advise you to contact Rev. Pato Messi.

You have to contact him directly on this information:

JOAKIN COMPENSATION HOUSE

REV. PATO MESSI

Email: revpatomessie88@live.com

Phone: +234 8020 665 049

- -

They both agreed there were a lot of errors in the language, spelling and typing. Again, there was no connection that Rev. Temple had with these people so it was obviously an attempted scam. Rev. Temple brought two more on the screen to check since Roger seemed interested.

- -

My dear beloved in the Lord:

My name is Mrs. Rita Chenkov. I am married to late Dr. Yuri Chenkov who was an oil merchant and international businessman before he died in the year 2001 after a brief illness that lasted for only five days. Before the untimely death of my husband we were both born again Christians. When my late husband was alive he deposited the sum of ($18,000,000.00 USD) with a Bank in UK whose name is withheld until we open up communication. Following my ill health, my doctor told me that I may not last for the next couple of months due to my cancer problem, the one that disturbs me most is my inability to move around and having known my condition I decided to donate this fund to a God fearing person that will utilize this money the way I am going to instruct herein, according to the desire of my late husband before his death. I don't want a situation where this money will be used in an ungodly way. I am not afraid of death hence I know where I am going. I know that I am going to be in the bossom of the Lord. Exodus 14:14 says that "the lord will fight my case and I shall hold my peace."

I don't need any telephone communication in this regard because of my health hence the presence of my husband's relatives around me always. As soon as I receive your reply, I shall give you the contact of the Bank where you shall reach them and I will also issue you a letter of authorization from the high court of justice that will prove you to be a beneficiary of this fund. Any delay in your reply will give me room in sourcing another individual for this same purpose.

Please endeavor to contact me with this email address:

Ritachenkov01@yahoo.com.uk

Your beloved sister in the Lord,

Mrs. Rita Chenkov

- -

OLIVIA FOUNDATION is offering loans to prospective customers at a reduced interest rate.

For more information about how to apply for the loan please contact:

Contact Person: Lady Olivia Smith E-mail: foundation.olivia@gmail.com

There is a prospect in my office worth $3.4 million for our benefit. I'll send you photos and ID for you to know me. For detail contact me with your name, phone number and address.

- -

"Say, I have needed a loan for $3.4 million," laughed Roger.

"Not sure where this one will go," joined in Rev. Temple. "This must be one of those to get your identity, but we know it isn't legal as she is trying to get you to work with her in this office or something."

Rev. Temple clicked on another one about a special lottery in Germany. The two focused on the screen as they saw several new things. This time the sender had typed it in bold face and it really jumped off the monitor. The two men were quickly drawn into the details as they read the bold print.

"I'm going to have to go," said Rev. Temple as he prepared to turn the computer off.

"Of course you do," responded Roger as he realized how much time he had been there. "I'm sorry I have taken so much of your time, but I do very much appreciate your agreeing to take me to the bus terminal."

"See you at 4 tomorrow afternoon."

"Ah—, we will miss him if we go then," said Roger. "He arrives at 6:30 a.m."

Rev. Temple's eyes widened. He yanked his head around and looked directly toward Roger with an opened mouth. Surely Roger was joking but there was no sign of a smile or laugh in Roger's face.

"Afraid you are right," laughed Roger. "The bus arrives at 6:30 in the morning and we need to leave at no later than 4:30 a.m. I'm really sorry, but that is the first bus and he will have been on it all night. I couldn't believe those buses stop that many times between Colorado Springs and Kansas City."

"Ok, I'll pick you up tomorrow morning and we will be on our way by 4:30. Now what is your address so I can pick you up?"

"I don't live that far from you. I'll just wheel over to you to save time getting on our way."

"Hey, that doesn't tell me where you live. You promised to tell me if I take you."

"Ha, ha, ha," laughed Roger. "We haven't been to the bus terminal yet. You can take me home though and then you will know."

Rev. Temple's right eyebrow went up in a questioned expression. He wondered what Roger would have him involved with next.

CHAPTER EIGHT

At 4 a.m. Dollie got out of bed to see who was in her kitchen rattling around. There she found an already dressed Rev. Temple slurping a bowl of cereal and buttering toast at the same time. As she came in the room the doorbell rang at the front door.

"What are you doing?" asked Dollie as her attention followed Rev. Temple as he quickly walked past her and answered the door. "Rather early to have company too."

Rev. Temple signaled Roger that he would be out in a second and then turned to Dollie. Smiling Rev. Temple told her he would be back around noon if all went well.

"All went well?" she questioned. "What does that mean? And who have you got out there? Is that Roger again?"

"Yes," said Rev. Temple as he reached for his jacket and slipped his feet in his shoes. "We are headed to Kansas City to the bus station."

"Bus station? Is Roger going somewhere?" she continued to question. "Hey, come back here Jack. What are you two doing?"

It was too late. They were both gone and she waved to the car as it headed down the street north to the major highway. There was a slight mist coming down as they got to the intersection and worked their way on to the ramp leading to the interstate.

"I don't think I have ever seen this few cars on the road," said Rev. Temple as he opened the conversation with a yawn. "You may have to talk to me to keep me awake. I didn't get to bed as early as I should have. I was at the Preacher's Alliance Meeting. It ran rather long. Something about the new man on the city council wanting to ban Christian symbols in front of the churches at Christmas and other religious holidays."

"I bet that got to be a hot little meeting," spoke up Roger. "Seems like the world is out to eliminate all signs of Christianity."

"Some of the preachers keep saying that 'separation of church and state' thing and that the founding fathers meant for Christianity to be a private thing. Well, yes, they didn't want the government to oversee religion but they sure didn't want it eliminated. Nearly every signer of the Declaration of Independence can be quoted demonstrating their strong faith in God. Bibles were sent with missionaries to the Indians by the government. The buildings in Washington, D.C. all have Scriptures displayed."

"I remember while I was in Iraq the last time that there was some movement to eliminate the chaplains. There was also an attempt to get them to not pray in the name of Jesus or use his name. What kind of religion is that?" added Roger.

"Sometimes I wonder if some of the preachers in town believe in God the way they talk," said Rev. Temple. "Don't quote me on that. Sorry, I shouldn't have said that, but it is so discouraging. We should be united in defending the faith. The idea of discussing how to eliminate it from public view is absurd."

As they drove into the city, the sun slowly began to appear behind them developing streaks of pinks, purples and oranges in the sky. The skyscrapers glistened as they reflected the rays from the rising sun. It made the city look especially beautiful. The trees were also striking as their autumn colors were bold and vibrant with the new sun of the day. The two men remained quiet as they took in the sights.

Rev. Temple turned down Broadway and worked his way to where he thought the bus terminal was located. He signaled and turned in the circle drive taking the closest parking space to the front door of the station. He helped Roger with his wheel chair and got him seated in it. In a matter of seconds they rolled to the front door of the terminal noting the lack of people in the parking lot and surrounding area.

"The door is locked?" said Rev. Temple.

"It's not quite 6 a.m. They will probably open soon," responded Roger. "See the sign over there?"

Once again the two of them turned and looked at the view of the city. They nodded at each other without saying a word. There was the sound in the distance of a morning bird singing its song. For that moment they were filled inside with a good feeling. It was a breath taking moment. Everything seemed right with the world. The mist had stopped and the air was fresh and crisp. There was a slight fog rising around the Missouri River Bridge making it look mystical. It was beautiful.

In all too short a time the sound of the bird was lost in the roar of the early morning traffic making its way to the businesses throughout the downtown. The sound of a siren was heard as a faint stream of smoke was seen rising several blocks away. The sound of a train whistle was heard near the river and the clanging of the freight cars being locked together. The world had come back to life after a night of rest.

A taxi drove in the parking lot and unloaded two older women in the 'no parking' zone just as three other cars wheeled in and parked. Car doors and the setting down of suitcases could be heard along with voices. Behind the two men a loud clicking sound was heard as the doors were unlocked. In a matter of seconds the entire terminal was alive with noise and people working their way to the ticket windows for information. The smell of hot coffee drifted throughout the waiting room.

Roger pointed to the arrival time chart as he rolled his chair toward it. He spotted the words "Colorado Springs" and ran his finger across the chart to where the time was listed. It read "6:30 a.m.—ON TIME."

Rev. Temple glanced at his watch and in his mind tabulated and was relieved that he could easily be back to the church to meet with the ladies in a special meeting he had set up for 2 p.m. He remembered how he had talked to a half dozen people individually on the phone and others in his office. They had expressed desires to bring God's vengeance on the people who the ladies had tried to help. One woman suggested that the ladies should gather bags of garbage they had at home and take them and dump them in the yards of the people that had been so disrespectful. Rev. Temple knew that would be a huge mistake. He knew he needed to get back in time to talk to them about what God would have them do and prevent them from doing anything outrageous.

Roger tapped Rev. Temple's hand and pointed at the bus pulling in the station. It displayed "Colorado Springs" on the marquee above the front window. Roger was getting nervous. He was about to meet the internet stranger named Lance. He wondered what Rev. Temple would think if Lance got off the bus and called him "master" or hugged him. Then he wondered what he would do with Lance as he had no idea where his father was or if he even knew the man. He questioned himself as he stood there waiting for the bus to unload.

"What will Rev. Temple think," he thought to himself. "What was I thinking arranging for him to come here?"

The people started filing off the bus. The first person was an African-American wearing a University of Hawaii sweatshirt. His hair had been shaved off and he wore gold earrings in both ears. The next person was dressed with an orange and green sweater, tight Levi jeans, and stocking cap. He looked like he had been on a ski trip. The next three to exit the bus were older women dressed in clothing reflecting Middle Eastern culture. Another woman, younger and pregnant, edged slowly down the bus steps and was immediately hugged by a man in uniform. The serviceman picked her up and carried her into the bus station. Finally, a young man approximately the age that Lance said he was stepped off the bus. Roger looked at him and approached him. On closer inspection, Roger was convinced it wasn't Lance.

Roger suddenly realized he didn't know for sure what Lance looked like. Although Lance had sent pictures there was no guarantee they were his pictures. Even if they were his photographs they might have been taken several years ago. What if his hair was different as he could have dyed it? In the pictures his hair looked frosted and highlighted. What if he had a beard or moustache? What if he had gained weight? On the other hand, if he really was doing without food what if he was severely underweight? There were a host of things that could change his appearance.

"Do you see him?" asked Rev. Temple.

"I don't think so," replied Roger. "There must be some more to get off."

They waited a while and when other people started getting on the bus Roger rolled over to the bus driver and asked if that was all that were getting off the bus. The bus driver nodded affirmatively and Roger looked at Rev. Temple with a puzzled look.

"Sir, would you check to make sure as someone could have fallen asleep and is still on the bus?" asked Roger.

"Afraid that is all there is," laughed the bus driver.

"So where is Lance?" Roger said out loud.

"Lance?" said Rev. Temple with a raised eyebrow. "Did you say Lance? Isn't that the guy that wrote that scam letter to me? You took the picture of his father home with you and promised to throw it away if you couldn't remember anything. Oh? You didn't?"

"Well," began Roger, "his father looked like an old friend of mine and so I did contact him and well, sort of—ah, sent him some money for food and then money to take the bus today."

Rev. Temple rolled his eyes. Despite the conversations the two of them had during the past week, Roger had been drawn in by the smooth talking Lance. As Rev. Temple looked Roger over he decided perhaps he should be supportive of Roger right now. He could see Roger looked embarrassed yet still had a desire to see Lance and to find out who the man in the picture was.

Rev. Temple went to the ticket desk and asked if there was a way to check to see if Lance had gotten on the bus or if he had missed a transfer somewhere along the way. The manager reported there was no way to check for those things. Both Roger and Rev. Temple were surprised having flown on planes where security measures are so strict. The ticket agent reported that there were no government regulations on the use of buses except to sell the ticket.

"So what do we do now," asked Rev. Temple as he looked at Roger.

"There is another bus at 11:30 a.m. He might be on it," said the ticket agent. "He would be able to use his ticket for the next bus as well. All he would need to do is exchange it with the agent."

"Do you mind if we stay for it?" requested Roger.

Looking at his watch and remembering the ladies meeting Rev. Temple felt the back of his neck getting tighter. Reaching for his cell phone he looked at Roger's face and knew somehow they needed to stay.

"Hello, Dollie?" began Rev. Temple.

"Is that you Jack," replied Dollie Burgess. "Where are you? Are you still with that Roger guy?"

"Yes, Dollie, I'm still with Roger. Can you go to the ladies' meeting at the church for me?" requested Rev. Temple. "It is at 2 p.m. and you know what the situation is. Someone urgently needs to calm them down and keep them from doing something stupid. Can you do that for me?"

"Why aren't you going to be here?" Dollie questioned.

"Something has developed here and I need to stay for a few more hours," Rev. Temple said hoping she would be satisfied without asking more questions.

"So, where are you?" continued Dollie.

"Ah," paused Rev. Temple. "Roger and I are here at the Kansas City Bus Terminal. His friend apparently missed the first bus and we are waiting for the second one."

"Oh," said Dollie sounding somewhat relieved. "That is too bad. I'm sure things will work out and don't worry about the ladies. I'll go over and we'll map out a better plan of helping the neighbors."

"Thanks, I owe you."

Rev. Temple turned to Roger and patted him on the back. Roger stared at the floor and shook his head back and forth mumbling to himself about being really stupid.

"I can stay," he began. "We are here and let's get this finished. He may have missed the first bus and took a later bus. Is there another besides the 11:30 bus?"

"Yes, there is a 5:30 p.m. bus," said Roger meekly.

"5:30? Let's hope he is on the 11:30 bus," laughed Rev. Temple. "Care for some brunch or have you had breakfast yet?"

The two of them went a block south to "Der Essen Platz" a rather unique German style restaurant with all sorts of German specialties available. They laughed as they ordered food using Roger's sketchy German to figure out what the menu said. As they waited for their food it gave Rev. Temple time to ask questions about this stranger in the wheel chair.

Since arriving at Sassafras Springs and the Nickerson Street Church, Rev. Temple had noticed the bearded fellow entering the sanctuary and rolling down to "his spot" every Sunday morning just as the opening song was being sung. There he would sit until the benediction began. Not waiting for the end of it Roger would move toward the door and by the word "Amen" have disappeared on his way down the sidewalk to his home.

As they ate the delicious crepes with strawberries and poached eggs on the side, Rev. Temple persuaded Roger to share information about his military service. It was an impressive story that was revealed. Roger had served for 20 years as a special unit ranger. Although living a regular life most of the time he would be called to be at the airport and be flown to special missions in a minute's notice. He was in the first group to enter Iraq as his group surveyed the situation and prepared for the entry of American troops. He was there when the leader of the country was captured and again was in Afghanistan on a special mission to locate major warehouses of ammunition. His tour of duty in these countries was very risky and lasted until the mission was completed. He reported that he missed the excitement and the feelings that came from knowing you were making a difference. He slapped his legs and commented about how miserable it was to be stuck in the chair and not able to serve any more.

Rev. Temple gained a deep appreciation for the servicemen and the risks they take to provide freedom and safety in the United States as he listened intently to the experiences Roger had lived first hand. Roger told about things that most Americans could never imagine. Rev. Temple quickly learned how horrible their job is and the sights they see that will last a lifetime in nightmares and emotional trauma.

Finally the 11:30 bus arrived and getting off was a troop of a dozen girl scouts on their way to a special meeting at Kemper Auditorium. There were also a couple of ladies, but that was it.

"Can't you call Lance and see where he is or what has happened?" questioned Rev. Temple.

"Afraid I don't have his phone number or his address," responded Roger.

"How about a last name? Maybe you can get his phone number from the yellow pages or operator."

"Afraid I don't know his last name either," said a frustrated Roger.

"I thought you said he was the son of a friend of yours?" sternly said Rev. Temple staring in his eyes.

"Yeah," began Roger, "about that—ah, I'm sorry."

Rev. Temple agreed to stay for the night bus and loaded Roger in the car and took him to the Truman Library for a tour. A visit to the oval office replica was impressive and sparked a good deal of conversation about the presidents in recent years.

"What ever happened to the belief that 'the buck stops here?'" said Roger.

The third bus arrived without Lance aboard and the two made their way back to Sassafras Springs. It was a quiet ride home. When they arrived Roger gave directions to his house and requested that Rev. Temple stay while he tried to find Lance online. Roger was eager to get information on what had happened. Rev. Temple apologized but said he needed to get home to see what Dollie had to say about the ladies' meeting. Bidding a good night Rev. Temple left.

Roger quickly turned on the computer and waited for the slow dial up to allow him to get online. Remarkably, there was Lance waiting and frantically typing words about how he had tried to get his ticket.

"Slow down," requested Roger. "You aren't making sense. What happened?"

"I went to get my suitcases and the door was locked," Lance replied.

"Door was locked," questioned Roger. "What door?"

"Yes," continued Lance in a panic. "I pounded on the door and it wouldn't open."

"Of course it won't open if you pound on it," muttered Roger wondering how stupid this kid could be. "Now what door are you talking about?"

"You don't understand."

"You are right. I don't understand. I sent money to buy a ticket so you could come here and you are saying you can't get a door open. Do you mean the door to your condo," said Roger with anger beginning to build. He was convinced he had been scammed as he read the confusing words of Lance. Roger knew he should have listened to Rev. Temple from the start. All that money he had sent Lance was wasted. Roger felt like such a fool. He was certain that nothing Lance could say now would pull him back into this obvious scam.

"I had bought the ticket and placed it in my suitcase," began Lance as he tried to explain. "I had some money left so I went to the restaurant on the corner. I knew I would probably not have much chance to eat on the bus. I put the suitcase with my ticket in the condo at the front door ready to pick up when I was ready to go to the bus terminal."

Roger shook his head thinking Lance had probably used the entire $90 for a steak dinner and wine. He was convinced the boy was one big rip off and felt anger inside that he had been taken in and especially after Rev. Temple had warned him. He expected Lance to now say he needed another $90 for the ticket.

Twelve hours he had bothered Rev. Temple about this scam artist. Roger kicked himself mentally as he relived the entire day being humiliated at the failure of Lance to get off each of the three buses. He grimaced at how he had gotten Rev. Temple to come at 4 a.m. and gotten home at nearly midnight.

"How stupid can I be?" sighed Roger as he stared at the computer.

Lance started his story trying to make it clear to Roger what had happened. Lance told how he had bought the ticket and put it in his suitcase. When he went back to get it the landlord had changed the locks to the condo and Lance could not get his bag. After pounding on the door enough to bring the manager, Lance tried to persuade the man to open the door. The manager explained there was $300 owed and he had noticed that Lance was about to leave. The manager wanted to make sure he got his money before allowing Lance to leave so had changed the locks and would not allow Lance back in the condo until the bill was paid—$300 back rent.

"I've been online all day trying to contact you," typed Lance. "Where have you been?"

"Where have I been?" laughed Roger. "You stupid, ah, a-hum."

Roger tried to regroup from his anger and looked the situation over. Was Lance telling the truth? Or was this another ploy to get more money as Lance was definitely headed toward asking for $300. That was obvious.

Roger shrugged his shoulders. "So what do I do?"

CHAPTER NINE

Rev. Temple was hard at work in his office typing his sermon for the next Sunday when he stopped and thought about Roger. Shaking his head he got up from the desk and stood looking out the window.

He saw a group of young boys headed to the park with a basketball. He could hear them laughing and the bouncing of the ball on the pavement. They stopped for a moment and appeared to be talking to someone across the street. Rev. Temple leaned forward to see who it was. There was no surprise. It was a group of girls heading toward the park with Angela and her Saint Bernard leading the way.

That brought a smile to his face. He thought about the youth group meeting three nights earlier and how hard it was to get the boys and girls to work together. They were all very shy except for a couple.

The junior high students were working their way thru puberty and here it was displayed as the two groups approached flirting from different angles. The boys demonstrated their sports ability with muscles and acting in control. The girls smiled and tossed their hair back in ever so graceful ways as they chatted and teased the boys.

"If life was always so simple," laughed Rev. Temple as he continued to watch. "On the other hand, when a teenager it isn't simple. Life is never simple no matter the age or the circumstances."

He reflected on the trip to Kansas City with Roger. He shook his head again and looked away from the window and back to his desk.

"I thought I had helped him and instead I gave him photographs and an email that inspired him to go ahead and become involved in a scam," thought Rev. Temple. "What could I have done to get the message into his mind and actions instead of leading him to get more deeply involved with a stranger?"

Rev. Temple paced back and forth thinking about the situation. He felt responsible for the actions of Roger yet how could he have known that Roger would take the picture or make contact by copying the email address while Rev. Temple was busy elsewhere.

Rev. Temple returned and sat down at his desk as he thought about the sermon. He had decided to share some things on the danger in life using the computer and the evil that lurks within.

"Perhaps someone will be listening and heed the warning," he said just as a crash was heard in the church parking lot. He jumped up and looked out the window.

There was a group of women huddled around a wagon loaded with gardening equipment, paint cans and a number of other items. In the group was Dollie who was waving a sign and appeared to be giving out orders as the women took things off the wagon.

"Now what?" said Rev. Temple as he turned the computer off and made his way to the parking lot.

"Alice," yelled Dollie, "you take that basket of petunias and a small shovel. I'll follow you with the red sage and the bag of fresh dirt. We'll get this planted before they know what hit them."

"Dollie?" interrupted Rev. Temple. "What is all this?"

"Isn't this great," replied Dollie Burgess. "We are helping people again today. Our meeting yesterday stirred us to want to do good for people even when they don't want it. We are going to force our good deeds on them. That's what God would want us to do."

Rev. Temple stood there with his mouth open. He had expected Dollie to help curb this excessive and destructive helpful attitude of the women's group. Instead she had become the leader for doing more.

"I'm glad to see your desire to help people," said Rev. Temple in a controlled calm voice as he worked to keep from saying they were all out of their minds. "Would you pause for a moment? I need to talk to all of you."

The ladies put their equipment down and surrounded Rev. Temple. They all stood there in their work clothes, hair done up in bandanas, displaying smiles and sparkling eyes. He had not seen a bunch so enthusiastic since telling the youth group they were going to take a trip to the lake for an overnight swimming party. He searched his mind looking for the right words to say.

"The church has been getting phone calls from neighbors complaining about being harassed," he began. "Officer Hays came by and informed me the church might get a summons to appear in court with charges of attempting to take advantage of the elderly in the community."

"Rev. Temple," said Dollie in an ugly tone. "We did only good things. We painted, cleaned, cleared trash, pulled weeds and many other things. Where is that wrong? We worked hard to help these people."

The ladies joined in with "Yes!" and mumbled among themselves. They looked at each other to feed each other's determination. As they did this they began to express the hurt and disappointment from not being thanked or appreciated for the kind deeds they had done. They looked at Rev. Temple waiting for him to provide encouragement instead of this negative talk he was giving. He had been their inspiration to help the neighbors.

"Didn't you preach just last Sunday," reminded Colleen Marx, "do unto others as you would have them do unto you?"

"Yes I did, but—," began Rev. Temple to respond.

"Well, there you are!" said Colleen Marx with a firm determined voice. "They want us to treat them like the mean spirited people they are."

"Colleen! You don't mean that," quickly replied Rev. Temple. "Think about what you said."

"We tried to do good things for them. I say get the dump truck ready and let's fill their yard with cow manure!" she shouted.

"Wait!" called Rev. Temple as the ladies stormed off.

"That didn't go so well," quietly said Dollie as she remained the only one standing next to Rev. Temple.

"Dollie," grimaced Rev. Temple. "What happened yesterday in the meeting? I counted on you with your wisdom and leadership ability to calm them down and focus them in a good Christian direction."

Dollie looked away.

"Well?"

Dollie looked down and avoided looking at Rev. Temple in the eyes. She appeared nervous and embarrassed. She realized she had failed to help Rev. Temple with something that she would normally be able to do.

"An explanation can be given me later but right now we need to follow the women and keep them from getting cow manure," said Rev. Temple frantically. "You don't think they really would, do you?"

Dollie laughed at the thought and then turned away as she remembered the discussion the ladies had the day before. Apparently that topic had been raised and one lady commented she had plenty available if the ladies wanted to use it.

"Ah, Rev. Temple," Dollie began, "perhaps we should go by Ethel Wall's."

Rev. Temple looked at Dollie and could see a slight twitch in her left eye. He raised his eyebrow at her and she nodded. He knew now that cow manure was on the agenda and they had better hurry before the church got arrested for the actions of this renegade ladies group.

Meanwhile Roger Brown was at his computer. As he opened email after email he was finding other scams sent to him. It was like answering the one scam to Lance with a financial response had opened a flood gate of others. He glanced down the list and determined he had received over forty.

He looked at the names on them and picked one. He clicked on it and opened it.

++

Dearest Friend,

I want to bring to your knowledge of a very lucrative business opportunity that I have. Well I work as an agent that accompanies contractors funds to be paid to them i have this deal and i won't mind you in it if you promise to keep optimum confidentiality.

The consignment consists of two boxes, the boxes contains about $20million all in $100.00 bills this money was accompanied by me to U.S.A and was handed over to a diplomat. The name of the Diplomat will be given to you as soon as you indicate your interest.

You will Call the diplomat and tell him that you are calling on behalf of Mr. George Padmore that handed the consignment to him, Also ask him how much it will cost to clear out this consignments, bear in mind that he is not aware of the content of the boxes, it was registered as CONFIDENTIAL DIPLOMATIC DOCUMENTS, you know that this consignment has been there for the past 2 month where I am looking for a trust worthy person to get it out.

This money was meant for the contractors that executed their contracts bear in mind that i am ready to release 40% of the total money to you for your help; I will be expecting your reply today and also a call on (+44) 7024041874 and please send to me your phone and fax number if interested.

Please direct your reply to my personal mailing address for security purpose. (linkgeorgepadmore@gmail.com)

Regards,

Mr. George Padmore
(+44) 7024041874

++

Roger shook his head as he thought about how foolish he had been to send money to Lance. He felt embarrassment again over getting Rev. Temple to go to Kansas City at 4 a.m. and waiting all day for the inevitable results of no Lance. And here was another scam—one of millions that were sent to poor unsuspecting people throughout the world.

"Lance," laughed Roger, "no more. You will get nothing from me now. I am on to you."

"Buzz!"

Roger jumped as he heard the sound of the computer "buzz" and knew it was Lance. He quickly turned his full attention toward the keyboard and clicked to see the message from Lance.

"You buzzed?" Roger typed sarcastically.

"Yes Sir.

"And how is my good friend Lance tonight?" said Roger gritting his teeth. "How much money you want tonight?"

"I'm not feeling fine sir," he replied.

"Oh?"

"Are you still there sir?"

"I think I'm here. Were you out for lunch?" said Roger.

"Buzz!"

"I'm here," quickly replied Roger. "Now quit pushing that buzzer!"

"Are you there sir? I'm here now master."

"What is with you?" said Roger. "Yes, I'm still her Lance and stop calling me Master."

"Okay master, Sir."

"You aren't responding to my answers. Are you not getting my typing?" asked Roger.

"I'm not happy here sir. How is everything over there sir?" grieved Lance.

"Things are quite nice here. Problem?"

"I want to be with you," begged Lance. "What can I do?"

"What did you do with your bus ticket?" asked Roger.

"I can't get it until I pay the $300 to the landlord. Then I can be on my way to join you. I'm so unhappy Sir. You tried to help me and I messed it up, Sir."

Roger paused and thought things over. Ok, the boy who had lived in another country and was humiliated as a slave probably couldn't think clearly and apparently is panicked about not having a master.

"So what if he is the son of a former friend or person I worked with?" thought Roger.

Roger made a quick call to the bus station in Colorado Springs and found that all Lance needed to do was trade his ticket in for a new one. Once Roger knew that he quickly turned his attention to Lance.

"Lance, I'm wiring you $300 to pay the rent. Once you get your luggage and the ticket go directly to the station and trade the ticket in for a new one. I want you on your way here as soon as possible. Have you got that?"

"Yes, Sir."

"I expect to find you on the bus tomorrow morning at 6:30."

Roger rolled his wheelchair down the street toward Western Union again. As he went he thought, "So how do I get Rev. Temple to take me to the bus station again? And how is he going to respond to my sending money again and again and again. I'm not even sure how I'm reacting to all of this, but I'm sure I know Lance's father. Why can't I remember who he is?"

CHAPTER TEN

"Was that Ethel we just met in the truck?" asked a slightly panicked Rev. Temple.

"It may have been," responded Dollie Burgess. "It did look like her. Why would she be driving the truck?"

They both looked at each other wide-eyed as Rev. Temple braked and worked to turn the car around.

"Think Dollie," demanded Rev. Temple. "Where would they take manure first?"

Dollie had her hands holding both sides of her face as she worked to remember all the remarks the ladies made at the meeting. Rev. Temple wiped the beads of sweat coming out on his forehead. Dollie shook her head slowly in disbelief that the ladies would actually dump manure on someone's yard.

"Think!" insisted Rev. Temple. "Think! Who did they talk about the most in terms of the bad reaction to their helping?"

"They were pretty excited about a number of people who treated them badly. Colleen said that Justin McGorney even chased them and took swings at them with a baseball bat."

"McGorney?" repeated Rev. Temple. "I don't know him. Where does he live?"

"A few blocks from the church," Dollie responded. "You know that old Victorian house that needs a paint job and has a yard filled with weeds."

Rev. Temple strained to remember the house Dollie was describing. He went down the streets in his mind checking off house after house that didn't fit her description. Finally like a light bulb coming on his eyes lit up.

"Oh, you mean the one with that purple trim," said Rev. Temple.

"No," replied Dollie. "That is Georgia Maddox. She was pretty abrasive in her comments to the ladies from what I hear. They are both on the hit list."

"Hit list!" exclaimed Rev. Temple. "You actually put together a hit list?"

Rev. Temple and Dollie looked at each other again and shook all over. Rev. Temple turned left and aimed toward the church building. He was hoping the ladies were meeting at the church first and that would give him an opportunity to stop them.

As he rounded the corner Dollie let out a scream when a blaring siren sounded behind them. Rev. Temple glanced in the mirror and saw Officer Herb Brown's red lights flashing and him motioning to pull over. Rev. Temple quickly slowed the car down and pulled to the side of the road. Officer Brown got out of his car and slowly walked to the side of Rev. Temple's car.

"Rev. Temple?" began Officer Brown. "I don't believe I have ever seen you break the law. Just the other day I commented that it was rare to find a minister who actually obeyed the speed limits."

"Officer Brown," began Rev. Temple, "we are in a bit of a hurry."

"Yes," laughed Officer Brown. "Aren't we all. So how fast do you think you were going?"

"Herb, I'm sorry about breaking the law but we were trying to stop some ladies who are going to cause a lot of trouble."

"Do tell," replied Officer Brown. "Dollie are you in on this scam to talk me out of giving a ticket?"

"Herb, you don't understand," began Dollie. "The ladies of the church have gotten a bit upset at some people in town and are in the process of preparing to dump manure in someone's yard—perhaps several people's yards."

"You are kidding," laughed Officer Brown.

"I wish we were, Officer Brown," continued Rev. Temple. "The ladies had wanted to do something nice for the neighbors of the church and had been trying to paint and clean up the yards of some of the elderly."

"And this is why you were racing down the street at 50 mph in a 35 mph zone?" said Officer Brown as he eyed them carefully while reaching for his ticket book.

"You don't understand Herb," said Dollie hurriedly. "The people responded badly to the help and threatened the ladies. The ladies in turn decided they wanted revenge and are planning to dump manure on the properties of those who hurt their feelings."

Officer Brown stood there with his mouth open. His eyes widened. He leaned toward the car and turned his head with one eye squinted and an eyebrow lifted.

"So where is this going to take place?" asked Officer Brown.

"We aren't sure and that was why we were going so fast," responded Rev. Temple. "We have to get there before the ladies do something stupid."

"Indeed," echoed Dollie.

Officer Brown took a deep breath and put the ticket book back in his pocket. He took one more look at Rev. Temple and Dollie Burgess and finally motioned for them to lead the way and he would follow.

In a few seconds the two vehicles were speeding into the church parking lot and circling around. After finding no signs of the ladies Rev. Temple asked Dollie to give directions to Justin McGorney's house. The two vehicles were quickly on the streets again with Officer Brown's siren going full volume and lights flashing. To pedestrians it appeared that Rev. Temple was trying to "out run" the police car and rumors were started immediately as cell phones were lifted and dialed to pass the word along that the preacher was a wild driver soon to be apprehended by Officer Brown—but that is how gossip goes in a small town.

The gossip was the least of Rev. Temple's worries right now. They had to find the ladies group and stop them before they did something really stupid. As the cars rounded the final corner on the way to Justin McGorney's house Dollie gasped. There was Ethel Wall's farm truck. It was an older dump truck capable of spreading manure all over McGorney's yard. It was backed up to the front porch.

Rev. Temple slammed on the brakes as he pulled the car to the side of the street. He jumped out shouting.

"Stop! Stop!" he yelled. "Don't do it!!!!"

Rev. Temple rounded the truck just in time to see the gate open and the manure begin to fall out. It poured out in huge amounts and landed on top of an unprepared and very surprised Rev. Temple. He had no chance to move.

Standing there completely covered in manure Rev. Temple looked pitiful. Dollie stood at the side shaking her head. Officer Brown covered his mouth to keep from laughing at the sight.

"Guess we were too late," said Dollie.

Rev. Temple looked at her and nodded as the manure dropped off of him little by little. He turned to the ladies now gathered at the edge of McGorney's porch who seeing Rev. Temple's condition realized how wrong and stupid their actions had been.

"Arrrrrrgh," came a loud screaming noise from the house. The ladies turned toward the door of the house and quickly retreated away from the house running as fast as they could. Justin McGorney with his baseball bat in hand came charging out of the door swinging it every direction. He was on the warpath now.

Rev. Temple still standing in the middle of the manure pile looked at Officer Brown who had his ticket book back out. Rev. Temple shook his head back and forth.

"This isn't going to be good for the church," he said aloud.

CHAPTER ELEVEN

The next morning Rev. Jack Temple once again took Roger Brown to the Kansas City bus terminal and once again Lance did not arrive on the three buses. Once again there was a very quiet ride home and once again Lance was eagerly waiting to talk to Roger when they returned.

"I need food to eat, Sir" began Lance.

"So where were you this time?" began Roger as he questioned Lance. "I was at the Kansas City bus terminal from 6 a.m. to 8 p.m. today. Why didn't you come? I believed in you."

"Sorry, Sir," replied Lance, "but I was arrested."

Roger dropped his mouth open. He sat there astonished at Lance's ability to draw him in to the situation. He had been ready to delete any messages and planned to refuse to talk to Lance but here Roger was once again listening to the on-going saga of Lance of Colorado Springs.

"How are you going to help me now, Sir?"

"What? Help you?" asked Roger.

"I need food. I'm sick I'm so hungry, Sir."

"First, Lance, I must know why you didn't arrive today," said Roger thinking there was no answer Lance could give that would satisfy him. Roger was not going to wire him any more money. He was determined that would not happen again.

"Sir, I went to the bus station and did what you said. I approached the ticket man and some guy came out and was leading me away. I thought he was arresting me and I put up a struggle."

"They arrested you? For what?"

"Well, it turned out they weren't arresting me but rather taking me to a different office to fill out papers on the transfer of the ticket. The man had a uniform and it made me think of the Gestapo in Argentina and I panicked. I guess I must have gotten rather wild as they called the police and then I was arrested."

Roger sat back away from the computer and rubbed his eyes. He sat there looking at the screen shaking his head and thinking about the situation.

"Then when they took me to the police station," continued Lance, "and asked questions of everyone involved they finally decided I was innocent of any crime and released me. Of course the bus had left by then."

"So why did you not take the next bus?"

"I had no ticket. They took it when I was being arrested. I asked for it back and no one could find it," revealed Lance.

"No ticket?" sighed Roger Brown. "Did you get the landlord paid?"

"Not exactly," replied Lance.

"Not exactly? What does that mean? What did you do with the money?"

"I paid the mechanic," continued Lance.

Roger had a big frown come across his face. His eyebrows twitched. He tensed.

"Mechanic?" asked a confused Roger. "Ah, where does he come into all of this?"

"He was repairing my truck."

Roger's head dropped. Gasping he typed a reply while trying to control his anger.

"You have a truck? Then why was I paying for a bus ticket?"

"I wasn't sure how you would react to paying for a mechanic so I used the bus money and the rent to pay for the repairs. Now I can drive to your place with my truck and I didn't want to leave it behind. I love my truck."

"So basically you lied about what you were going to do with the money the whole time?" said a depressed Roger thinking this was enough. He was sure now that he was not going to send more money to Lance. "I had a friend drive me to Kansas City to the bus terminal twice and spent the entire day both times waiting for you and you were lying to me?"

"If you would send me money for gas I can be there tomorrow and we can start planning on what I can do for you? I'm very excited about this. I've sent a picture of my truck. I hope you like it."

"You think I'm going to trust you to show up here if I send you money for gas to put in the truck?" said Roger.

Roger checked the emails and there was one from Lance. He opened it and was impressed. It was a good looking 4 wheel drive very shiny black truck probably a year old. He could see that Lance would love his truck. It was a beauty. He also thought it would come in handy to have Lance and his truck available to take him places.

"Ok, Lance, I'm sending you money for gas. I expect your truck to be in my driveway by tomorrow afternoon. Got that?"

"Got what?"

"Never mind," laughed Roger. "I'm wiring you the money and please get here. Don't let me down."

"Yes, Master."

"Hey," interrupted Roger. "You know I don't want you calling me master."

Roger paused for a minute. "If you were my slave you would follow my orders and so far you have not done that very well. It could be a big improvement if you think of me as your master. On the other hand, I am beginning to think that you were left by your master because he was going nuts trying to deal with you."

"No, Sir."

"So my slave," begin Roger, "I am ordering you to be here tomorrow. Get in the truck and drive here now."

"Yes, master."

"That's better," said Roger thinking he was going to make some progress.

"I'm following your orders but I'm not feeling good about the orders, Sir."

"What?" replied Roger, "You dare to question your Master's orders? Whether you feel good about the order or not—if I am your master you do what I say. Is that understood? Of course I would not ask you to do anything illegal or dangerous or bad. You can trust me to have you do only things that will help us both."

Roger turned off the computer and rolled to the door and out into the sunlight of the gorgeous day that was taking place outside his house. As he whistled along his way he suddenly stopped.

"Wait a minute!" he said aloud. "How did he do that? I wasn't going to send him money and here I am on my way to do it again. What is wrong with me?"

With a shrug of his shoulders Roger continued to Western Union and wired the money for gas. He then returned and typed in the confirmation number for Lance thinking to himself that he was the slave of Lance rather than the other way around.

Three hours later a phone call was received by Roger. It was the emergency room at the Colorado Springs Hospital. The nurse making the call reported that Lance had been injured in a truck accident and had stated that Roger Brown in Sassafras Springs was next of kin.

"So you are Roger Brown that is related to Lance Perez?" asked the nurse.

"I might be. What has happened? Is he alright?" questioned Roger Brown.

"Lance apparently was turning on I-70 and ran off a culvert on the side of the road. The highway patrol believes that he passed out. Lance reported that he had not eaten for a couple of days which contributed to the accident."

"How is he?" asked a concerned Roger as he felt guilty for not sending money for food.

"He will be released tomorrow," stated the nurse.

Roger leaped at the news. He now knew a place where he could meet Lance in person. He thought out a plan to fly to Colorado Springs to be at the hospital before Lance could leave. Here was a chance to find if

Lance was real or not. If he was real, Roger would bring him to Sassafras Springs.

As Roger began packing a suitcase the doorbell rang. He started to ignore it but saw through the window that Rev. Temple's car was parked in front. Roger rolled to the front door and opened it. There was Rev. Temple with a Super Supreme Pizza from Roselee's.

"Hi," began Rev. Temple. "Thought you might be hungry for some pizza. Is this a bad time? Are you going somewhere?"

Roger looked down as he rolled away from the open door. Rev. Temple entered and sat the pizza on the table. He turned and looked at Roger. Roger tried not to look at Rev. Temple's face. Guilt was swallowing him knowing he was continuing to contact Lance despite Rev. Temple's feelings on the matter.

"I thought you might be depressed," began Rev. Temple. "I know you had high hopes of helping this young man online but there are scams every day. This young man was just taking advantage of you. Believe me."

"Jack," said Roger weakly. "I consider you a good friend and not just my minister."

"Thanks, Roger," responded Rev. Temple. "I appreciate you saying that. Is there something you need to talk over with a friend?"

"I don't suppose you would like to take a quick trip to Colorado Springs? I will pay for it?"

"Oh gosh," gasped Rev. Temple. "What have you done now?"

CHAPTER TWELVE

Ten minutes later the two men were on their way to Colorado Springs. It was the opinion of Rev. Temple that this was the quickest and easiest way to convince Roger that he was making a mistake believing in this young man. He wanted to help Roger but all other efforts had failed. This seemed like the perfect solution. Despite the cost and the time it would consume once and for all Roger would have the opportunity to know for sure if Lance's story was real or a lie.

As they came to the edge of Sassafras Springs, flashing red lights and a siren pulled Rev. Temple to the side of the road. Roger and Rev. Temple both had puzzled looks on their faces as Officer Brown approached the car. Neither could think of anything that was illegal.

"Officer Brown," began Rev. Temple, "we meet again."

"Yes," said Officer Herb Brown while clearing his throat and working to keep the matter serious. "This is a bit different. I have a couple of things to give you. This is a court order banning any church member from coming in the yards of Justin McGorney, Georgia Maddox, Leon Cronhardt, Wilson Hughes, Rosemary Miller, Virginia Crow, and Mary Lou Metz."

"You're kidding," replied Rev. Temple as Roger squirmed to see the papers over Rev. Temple's shoulder.

"And this one is a summons to appear in court in 30 days for trespassing, destroying property, invading a person's privacy, harassment, and other smaller complaints."

Roger groaned as he watched Rev. Temple's brow wrinkle and his hands shake. Roger knew this was a good reason for Rev. Temple to cancel the trip and held his breath as Rev. Temple and Officer Brown continued to talk. This was serious trouble the church was in. Roger didn't know what had happened but when people in town start banning the church people from ever stepping on their property it sounds big.

"Thank you Officer Brown," said Rev. Temple. "I guess I shouldn't be surprised."

"Might have been avoided had I not stopped you for speeding yesterday," commented Officer Brown. "I will testify that you were racing to stop what the ladies were doing and that you were not directly involved in the actual vandalism."

"Vandalism?" echoed Roger.

"Thanks, Herb," calmly said Rev. Temple. "I appreciate that. As for now I'm on my way to Colorado Springs to solve another situation. My, it is exciting being a preacher . . . ."

Rev. Temple turned toward Roger and punched him in the arm as he said, "Hey, we have a scammer to catch so let's go!"

The two barreled down I-70 working their way thru rush hour traffic in Kansas City and through the treeless landscapes of Kansas. As they approached Colorado hundreds of huge windmills came into view. Like a science fiction movie the huge propellers slowly came into vision on the hills twirling round and round. The sight was somewhat spooky as it appeared the countryside was being taken over by aliens from outer space.

As they entered Colorado the temperatures began getting cooler as a storm was approaching. They could see it miles in front of them with lightning flashing and deep dark clouds rolling rapidly toward them. Further beyond that was the faint appearance of heavy clouds. They later found that to be the Rocky Mountains.

"I wonder if the storm clouds are giving us a warning of what we are about to get involved with once we find Lance," commented Rev. Temple.

Meanwhile at Porter's Place, the ladies had gathered to discuss their situation and to feed their stressed bodies with some of Ike's long johns and filled pastries. They were unaware of the court order banning them from going on properties or that the church was going to have to go to court and be fined for trespassing, vandalism and an assortment of other crimes.

"This doing 'good' for people is not quite what I expected," began Sherrie Bennett. "I was eager to do it and thought how wonderful it would be for the young people to be involved."

"Yeah," echoed Colleen Marx.

"I can't believe that McGorney guy," began Sarah Jenkins. "He called me old. That angry dirty old ugly man called me 'old' and I don't like it."

"He could hardly get off the porch despite waving that baseball bat around," continued Emily Houseman. "How dare he call us old!"

"I say we sneak over and put a cherry bomb under his porch," plotted Lori Calder. "My son has some left from the 4th of July."

"Now wait," interrupted Maggie Cushing. "Remember we got carried away earlier and dumped manure on Rev. Temple. I realize a good portion of that ended up in McGorney's yard but our plan wasn't to humiliate the preacher. I guess you know Jack ended up shoveling all of it back in the truck and apologizing to McGorney."

"It wasn't necessary to do that," criticized Sherrie Bennett. "Rev. Temple was wrong to clean up that mess. We put it there for McGorney."

In the corner of the room was Josh McDaniel, editor of the Sassafras Springs Gazette working on the editorial for the paper. He had listened quietly and finally decided to ask a few questions to find out why the ladies were so upset. He sensed that his good friend Rev. Temple was also involved in some way. He also saw that Rev. Temple would have bigger problems if these women continued making plans like he had just heard.

Josh McDaniel was always working to bring the community together. He filled the newspaper with meaningful and positive encouragement for projects in the community. Though not certain what the ladies had done it was apparent this situation needed a push in a better direction.

"Ladies, good evening," began Josh McDaniel. "What brings you here to Porter's Place this time of the afternoon?"

The ladies greeted Josh and all together started complaining about the attitude of people in the community toward receiving help. They told how they had graciously and with a wonderful Christian spirit approached a variety of homes to help improve their appearance. They told how they worked hard to paint, weed, and repair things at over a dozen locations only to be run off and threatened by the owners. They explained how they had taken homemade cookies and tried to show a caring spirit only to see the treats thrown in the wastebaskets.

"Well, you ladies have been treated terrible," smiled Josh McDaniel. "I think we should tar and feather those ungrateful people and drive them out of town if they won't praise you for being good little Christians."

The ladies first gave an "amen" and then got quiet. Silence filled the room for a couple of minutes. Ike came out from the backroom to see what was happening in his restaurant as it sounded like everyone had left. To his surprise the restaurant was still half full of ladies.

"What happened?" Ike asked.

The ladies looked at him and then at each other and then out the window. Ike looked at Josh who smiled and nodded that everything was alright.

"So, what would you do Josh," asked Maggie Cushing. "I know we got wrapped up in wanting to do something great for the community. Yes, we got carried away for sure when our feelings were hurt. I'm ashamed we lost control and dumped manure on McGorney's yard."

The ladies all nodded in agreement.

"What would you like to do?" asked Josh McDaniel.

"We would like to help these people keep their yards and houses looking nice," commented Sherrie Bennett. "It seemed like a simple thing. We had supplies and could actually do the work. The people were not to pay anything and we were volunteering. That's all it was."

"I see," responded Josh McDaniel.

"I guess we should have asked the owners before we went to work on their yards," offered Linda Morrow. "I think Rev. Temple told us that before he left and I know Dollie had said that when we met later."

"You didn't ask?" replied Josh McDaniel. "No wonder these people got upset. How would you like it if someone came on your property and went to painting your house or redoing your garden?"

"Actually," laughed Ike, "any time you want to weed gardens, mow lawns or paint the house come on over to my place and go to work. Don't even need to ask."

Josh gave a disapproving look toward Ike not wanting to break the train of thought. Josh explained to the ladies how the people they wanted to help were living on small incomes and didn't have money to use for things like paint or flowers. He agreed the concept of helping these people was a wonderful idea but that it must be understood that not all of them would want to be helped.

"Pride is an important thing for an older person," continued Josh McDaniel. "You take that away and these people won't have any desire to live."

The ladies were left by Josh to think about what he had said. He went to the newspaper office and before printing the newspaper took time to write a new editorial. In it he stressed the need to not only be a cheerful giver but to be a cheerful receiver when people strive to help.

"You know he is right," said Emily Houseman. "I sure wouldn't appreciate someone coming in my yard and ripping out flowers and things in my gardens. I take a great deal of pride in them. Despite not always having a weed less garden I am proud that I'm still able to work in them. All the garden food is special to me too. I like being able to share tomatoes and corn and green beans and zucchini with my neighbors."

"True," the ladies echoed.

"So what do we do?" asked Maggie Cushing. "Do we pick a missionary or continue with the plan to help people in town?"

Before the group could get a discussion going Dollie Burgess came in the door. She looked worried.

"Have any of you seen Jack?" said Dollie in an excited and worried voice.

"Rev. Temple is missing?" Sarah Jenkins asked.

"I don't know," said Dollie. "He and that Roger Brown—the one who is in the wheelchair that comes to church and sits over in the corner every Sunday—have made two trips to the Kansas City bus terminal this week. They left at 4 in the morning. Then I got home and found a note that he and Roger were on their way to Colorado Springs and would be back tomorrow. What is going on?"

CHAPTER THIRTEEN

Slowly, Rev. Temple drove passed house after house looking for 327 ½ E. Sandford Road. The two men had been to the Colorado Springs Hospital and found that Lance was dismissed a few minutes before they arrived. The nurse fortunately had given them an address of where Lance was supposed to live. When they arrived at the location they noticed it was a government office for social services with another section of rental rooms for immigrants.

"Seems like a reasonable place for Lance to be if he was from another country," began Roger, "though I suspect the apartments are intended for individuals who have just arrived in America. Oh, there is a man. Pull up beside him and let's ask him if he knows Lance."

"Excuse me, Sir," shouted out Rev. Temple. "We are looking for Lance Perez. Do you know him or where he lives?"

The stranger quickly ducked his head and ran down the street. Rev. Temple and Roger Brown looked at each other and shrugged their shoulders.

"Perhaps I need to get out and get a closer looks at the apartment numbers," said Rev. Temple. "I can't make sense out of them while driving around."

Rev. Temple parked the car and got out telling Roger he would come back for him if he found anything. Looking closer at the numbers on the buildings and above the doors Rev. Temple was more confused. The numbers on the buildings didn't follow any normal sequence. Some had letters in the address. None of the apartments had "1/2" in them. As Rev. Temple returned to the car Roger pointed toward one of the offices of the social service department. A lady was preparing to lock the door and leave.

"Excuse me," said Rev. Temple, "do you know Lance Perez?"

"Lance?" she responded. "No Lance Perez here that I know of."

"Thanks, sorry to have bothered you."

The lady locked her door and turned to walk down the street. Roger Brown pulled out a picture of Lance and called to her to look at the picture as she might recognize him. She stopped and took a good look at it.

"You say his name is Perez?" she questioned.

"We think so. His first name is Lance," replied Roger Brown.

She looked at it again and puzzled over it. She looked up and studied Rev. Temple and Roger closely. Then she nodded in the negative and handed the picture back to Roger.

"We were hoping to find him. I have been sending him money and he had a truck accident. He was in the hospital. I came to see him and to make sure he is alright."

"And you say his name is Perez?" she asked again.

"That is what the hospital said," responded Rev. Temple. "It could be something else as I think he was using an alias."

The woman took a deep breath and looked Rev. Temple and Roger Brown over again. She started to leave and then turned back.

"This picture looks more like Lance Simpson. He lives next to me in the condos three blocks down the street. Here, let me write the address down. He had been living in #3 at 719 Sandford. Those are nice condos. They have a great view of the mountains. I was in his condo when an older man was living there with him. I don't know what happened to the older man but Lance is still in the building. I found him sleeping in front of the door of his condo one night when I came home extra late. I asked him about it and he said he forgot his key and didn't want to disturb the manager."

"I thought you lived here," interrupted Roger.

"No," she replied. "I work in the social services department. My condo is on the same floor as Lance. I tried to get Lance to talk to me on several occasions but he avoided me. He often looks hungry and sick. With social services I know of government programs that might provide money for him if he qualified. I tried to get him to fill out a paper to request government assistance, but he wouldn't hear of it. I'm rather confused about him."

"Join the crowd," laughed Roger. "I am totally confused about him. He sent me a picture of his father who I'm sure I have known sometime in the past. Lance has given me a little bit of information at a time and everything seems to fit, but not enough to draw conclusions or to spark memories."

"Do you know where he might take a truck to be worked on if it was in an accident?" asked Rev. Temple.

"No problem with that one," quickly responded the girl. "He told me his truck was being worked on at Diamond Jim's Garage down the street that way 2 blocks."

"Did you see his truck or hear him say anything about it being in the shop recently?" asked Roger.

"Oh yes. He was panicked about paying for the truck a couple of weeks ago. It is a shiny black four wheel drive. Really a nice looking vehicle. He also mentioned something about going east to Missouri to a friend's house soon and that the truck needed to be in good shape to make the trip."

Roger looked up wide eyed and glanced at Rev. Temple. The girl expressed her farewells and said she needed to be getting home as she had company coming. She started walking down the street then turned back once again.

"I hope you can help him," she quietly said with concern in her voice. "He seems lost and alone."

Rev. Temple wrote some notes on a tablet and looked around to get a feel for the place.

"Roger," began Rev. Temple, "I apologize. Everything seems to be falling in place and this Lance person must be on the level. Of course we still have not found him. What do we do now?"

The two men wrote down the information they had and began analyzing it. They also contacted the highway patrol and were able to get a supporting statement about where and when and what happened in the accident that Lance reported to Roger. They drove to the mechanic's shop and actually got to see what they thought was the truck. The mechanic denied knowing a Lance Perez or Simpson or that the truck was his.

"That was strange," sighed Roger after they left the mechanic's shop. "I know that was his truck. It had to be. I have a picture and the license number is his. So why would the mechanic not tell us where Lance is?"

"I don't know but we need to get a room," said Rev. Temple. "It is getting late and we can't drive back to Sassafras Springs tonight."

"There is a motel across the street," pointed Roger Brown. "Why not get a room there and we can keep an eye on this place. We might see Lance before the night is over. From my conversations with him I feel sure he will be close by his truck."

"Did she say he slept in front of the door to his condo?" asked Rev. Temple. "That seems strange."

"Here is how I see it," began Roger. "Lance is lost in this town because the only person he knew was the man who he claims was his master. The man left him with nothing but a place to stay and a truck. Because of Lance's strange previous three years with this master he probably is unable to make decisions. He has no money to get a place to stay or food so he will go to the places that he can connect with. That would be the condo and his truck. He sleeps at the door since he can't get in the condo but still feels close to his master. He may even think that the master will come back some day."

"You think he will?" questioned Rev. Temple.

"No, not at all. He is gone and Lance is lost needing someone to help get him reconditioned into the world as a normal person. That is why I want to help him."

The two men checked into the motel and managed to convince the manager to give them a room where they were able to get a full view of the mechanic's shop. They ordered some Chinese food to be delivered and worked out a plan to keep 24-hour surveillance on the shop.

The hours passed slowly during the night. There was no activity at the mechanic's shop except the lights going on in the adjoining rooms which the two men decided was where the mechanic lived. At around 3 a.m. Rev. Temple on a hunch decided to return to the condos to see if Lance might have returned to sleep in front of the door again.

On the door was taped an envelope addressed to Master Dan. Rev. Temple pulled it off and opened the envelope. In it was a message telling Master Dan that Lance had driven to Missouri and was now living with a man named Roger Brown. He shared how nice Roger had been to him and that he was confident he would make an excellent Master and that Master Dan should not worry about him.

Rev. Temple stood there speechless. Could this Lance be telling the truth about all of this slave stuff and bringing him from Argentina to the USA? There were so many questions developing in Rev. Temple's mind now.

"What does this mean that he has driven to Missouri to be with Roger? The truck is at the mechanic's shop. When did he go to Missouri? Why didn't Roger get told this?"

Rev. Temple hurried back to his car and drove to the motel. As he opened the door Roger was up and ready to go as he had seen Lance pull out in the truck and head east. Rev. Temple shared the note he had found. The two of them hurriedly checked out of the motel and got on the road back to Sassafras Springs at 4 a.m.

CHAPTER FOURTEEN

Later that day Roger and Rev. Temple drove into Sassafras Springs having driven straight thru without stopping except for gas and restrooms. They immediately headed for Roger's house. They both ran inside with Roger clicking on the computer and typing the password. The two sat there waiting for Lance to come on the screen.

Meanwhile across town the ladies were gathered at Mr. McGorney's again. This time they had stopped at the street and Dollie Burgess approached the house. Mr McGorney slowly opened the screen door and looked at her with a mean scowl. Dollie quietly cleared her throat and began.

"Mr. McGorney, the ladies are deeply embarrassed at the terrible behavior they have shown the past week. We would very much like to apologize for invading your property and treating you disrespectfully. We hope you will accept our apology and forgive us. If there is anything we can do to make up for it please tell us now. If you want us to leave you alone we will."

"What kind of trick are you pulling now?" Justin McGorney asked looking at Dollie with a skeptical smile. "You think I'm going to drop that law suit. I plan to take you for everything that church is worth. When I get thru with you there won't be a Nickerson Street Church."

Dollie gasp but took a deep breath again and continued. She explained that she and the ladies were willing to work free to make up for their bad behavior. She asked if there was anything he would like them to do around the house or yard?

"We would like to demonstrate the serious manner in which we have approached this situation. We recognize that we have done some pretty evil things."

The ladies looked at each other and mumbled among themselves about what evil thing they had done but tried to look sincere as Dollie had insisted they do. They returned to standing still and being quiet. In that location they were staring at the peeling paint on McGorney's house. They were watching the back yard where McGorney had dumped bags of trash and set them afire. The ashes and remaining trash were now blowing over the neighborhood. The ladies were looking at the broken yard swing and the tangled vines that were the only thing keeping the swing from collapsing. There was no question that this man's yard was a disgrace for the entire neighborhood, but it was his to do with as he wanted.

"Is there anything we can do for you, Mr. McGorney?" concluded Dollie.

Justin McGorney stepped down off the porch. He walked to the corner of the house and took a good look at his yard. He looked at the ladies standing quietly at the curb. He turned around and confronted Dollie face to face.

"Yes," began Mr. McGorney, "I believe there is something you can do. I remember you Dollie. You were the first person to come to my house with a dessert when my wife died. You continued to return with other things. You always had an encouraging word. I will never forget that as it meant a lot to me and to my children."

Dollie thanked him and then said, "If you want us to leave you alone we can, but we really would like to do something for you. At Nickerson Street Church we care about people and it is a part of our ministry to reach out and help others. We don't mean to hurt anyone or insult or be disrespectful when we do that. Sometimes we do get carried away and overzealous in our efforts but our hearts are in the right place."

Mr. McGorney sat the baseball bat down on the front porch. He motioned for the ladies to come to him. He smiled and offered his hand as a truce or sign of friendship. He shook the hand of each one of them.

"I miss my wife," he began. "I really miss her and sometimes I get overly excited too. I get rough and mean to hide my grief. I'm sorry. I was out of line too. I had not touched any of the flower beds since my wife died as I looked at them as hers. It is time to clean them up and put some life back in this place. If you want to clean out the weeds and plant some flowers I'm all for it now. Let's bring some beauty back to this old place. My wife would like that."

The ladies applauded and Dollie quickly stopped them from jumping into work. She turned to him and asked, "What would you like for us to do?"

He smiled. He pointed to the yard swing and asked them to clear out the vines and get some paint, nails and replacement boards to repair it.

"That will be the first task. Let's see how you do?" he directed.

The ladies worked most of the day and left feeling very good about the work they had done to help Mr. McGorney. Another group of women went to the home of Mrs. Maddox where a similar scene developed. They too were able to leave with a good feeling inside their hearts. The youth group worked at four other houses with equally good results.

Rev. Temple and Roger Brown waited all afternoon for a response from Lance but nothing happened. Lance didn't come online. Finally Rev. Temple told Roger he had to return to the church to finish preparation of his sermons for the next day. Worn out and stressed Rev. Temple stopped at the doorway and turned again to Roger.

"Let's pray for Lance," said Rev. Temple. "It is in God's hands as we have done more than we should have. I suspect we are getting in the way of the plan God has in mind. Let's turn it over to him."

They prayed. Rev. Temple walked to his car and was getting in it when Roger shouted to him and said Lance was on the phone. Rev. Temple rushed back to the house.

"Where is he?" Rev. Temple quickly asked.

Roger looked puzzled. He shook his head. His mouth was open in disbelief. Rev. Temple took his arm and shook him to tell him what was going on.

"He says he has been kidnapped," began Roger.

"Kidnapped!" laughed Rev. Temple. "Where? Here in Sassafras Springs?"

"Yes," responded Roger in disbelief. "He says he stopped at Casey's to buy me something as a gift and when backing out of the parking lot hit a car. The people hearing his foreign accent got the impression he would disappear and they wouldn't get paid for repairing their car. So he says they have kidnapped him. They want $500 before they will let him go."

Rev. Temple sat down. Roger sat down next to him. They looked at each other in shock.

CHAPTER FIFTEEN

Rev. Temple got back to his apartment in Dollie's house around midnight having pulled an old sermon out and reshaped it to use for the Sunday morning service. Dollie was already in bed but had left a message on the kitchen table of things he could eat but he didn't stop to eat. He was too tired and stressed. He went directly to bed.

Meanwhile, Roger was studying the picture again. He was certain he knew the man in the picture standing in front of the castle. He pulled out some of his scrapbooks and looked thru some of the pictures from his months stationed in England. He tried to imagine the man at different ages. Perhaps the stranger had changed over the years. Roger found nothing to trigger a memory.

Next he pulled out scrapbooks from when he was stationed in Afghanistan. As he looked thru them he remembered the conversation he had with Lance. He shook his head at the insane comments about being kidnapped at Casey's in Sassafras Springs.

"There is no one in this entire town that would kidnap a person," sighed Roger Brown. "What kind of fool does Lance take me for?"

Then Roger laughed as he remembered all the money he had sent Lance over the past month. He stopped and totaled it up. He suddenly realized he had sent over $5000 and spent another $1000 getting to Colorado Springs and back plus the motel and food.

"How stupid am I?" laughed Roger again. "Well, Lance, you got nearly every penny I have. There isn't any more for you to get."

He clicked the computer on and started to delete everything about Lance. Just as he was about to finish came a loud "BUZZ" on the computer. He knew it was Lance. Did he dare talk to him?

"BUZZ"

"Ok, Lance I'm here. What do you want this time?" said Roger.

"These people are not nice. They have me locked in this room. They said I could use the computer to contact you but they are standing over me now and are giving me only a few minutes. Isn't there anything you can do? I'm scared."

"You can't be serious," sighed Roger. "I do not believe that you have been kidnapped. I do not believe you drove to Missouri and are here in Sassafras Springs. I'm through with you Lance. I can't afford any more money. I have nothing left. You took it all."

"Oh, Master," began Lance. "I'm so sorry. I didn't mean to hurt you or get you involved in something or take all your money. Master, I'm so alone and scared and hungry and . . . ."

Roger stopped looking at the screen. He yanked up the scrapbook from Afghanistan to throw it across the room in anger, but dropped it on the floor. Pictures went everywhere. He groaned as he looked at the mess. As he sat there in the wheelchair straining to reach the photographs he spotted one particular picture. He saw the man that he had been trying to remember. There was a man standing in camouflage clothes with a hard hat and work boots. Roger suddenly began remembering the man in the picture.

"It can't be," said Roger nearly in shock. "Jackson Simpson? Is this your son I've been talking to?"

Roger turned to the computer and started typing again. "Lance, I know your father. He saved my life when I was in Afghanistan eighteen years ago. Lance? Are you there? Did you hear me? Answer me. Tell me where you are or what I'm to do to get you free?"

There was no reply.

The next morning Rev. Temple made his way to Roger's to see if there was any news about Lance. There was no answer at the door which concerned Rev. Temple. He circled the house looking in windows and saw no activity. He finally left hoping Roger would be at church later.

When he turned the corner to drive in the parking lot at the church he was surprised to see a larger crowd than usual. There was Justin McGorney and Mrs. Maddox making their way to the front entry way. Rev. Temple rubbed his eyes and made his way to Dollie to find out what was going on. She briefed him on the previous day's success story.

He was once again reminded of the wonderful work that can be accomplished when the preacher has stepped out of the way. The ladies had accomplished their mission and the community apparently approved.

Officer Herb Brown drove up and motioned for Rev. Temple to come to the car. Officer Brown presented Rev. Temple with a letter dropping the charges against the church and explained that the issue was settled. Rev. Temple breathed a very big sigh of relief.

He looked up from reading the letter and was greeted by Josh McDaniel, editor of the newspaper.

"Josh," exclaimed Rev. Temple. "This is great to have you here!"

"I came because there is a pretty good story here with these ladies going around improving the properties of those in need. Don't you think?"

Rev. Temple coughed and nodded. He added that he was very proud of all of his members and hoped one day that would include Josh McDaniel.

As Rev. Temple watched Josh McDaniel walk to the entrance there was a tap on the back of his coat. He turned and looked down. There was Roger with a huge smile on his face.

"There you are," responded Rev. Temple. "I was worried when I didn't find you at home this morning. What news do you have for me?"

"I remembered who the man in the picture is. Once I figured that out I promptly started rolling my wheelchair up and down the streets trying to find the black truck."

"My word, Roger," interrupted Rev. Temple. "You didn't? You know Lance isn't here."

"Wrong, Jack," laughed Roger Brown. "I found the truck, called the police and we rescued Lance from the kidnappers."

Roger waved and motioned for a young good looking man to come join them and then said, "I want to introduce you to Lance Simpson, whose father, Jackson Simpson, saved my life in Afghanistan."

"Praise God!" joined in Rev. Temple. "You really know his father? Are you sure this is really his son?"

"Yes," laughed Roger. "I remember holding Lance several times when Jackson and I were on leave in Kenya. Lance was only three years old then. I had forgotten about that brief vacation in Kenya. I know this is Lance because I remembered a birth mark on his left foot. I insisted he show me before we did any more talking."

Lance smiled and nodded as he pointed to his foot that had the mark.

"Jackson and I didn't know each other long. He was an engineer on a project in Iraq and somehow he got on the wrong plane and was flown to Afghanistan. That was fortunate for me because as he was landing the plane it was a distraction that halted the attack by the Taliban. That brief break turned the battle in our favor and we were able to keep from being killed. He literally saved our lives."

Rev. Temple shook Lance's hand and welcomed him to Sassafras Springs. He then asked what the plan was as to where Lance was going to go. Would he stay with Roger or would they be able to find his father? Roger joyfully reported that he had already located Jackson and he was flying in that weekend.

As they entered the sanctuary, Rev. Temple smiled at the full house. It was full of people who had been fighting each other all week. Lawsuits, vandalism, anger, hurt feelings and mysterious events filled the lives of these people and now they sat under one roof. Unity had come because people cared and shared their gifts of honey. Not because of a sermon Rev. Temple had preached or because of his calling on a lot of different people. It was full because the people of the congregation were involved in witnessing to each other and showing they cared.